Stealing
Stacey

Also by Lynne Reid Banks

The Indian in the Cupboard
Return of the Indian
The Secret of the Indian
The Mystery of the Cupboard
The Key to the Indian

Angela and Diabola
Alice-by-Accident
The Dungeon

And for younger readers

Harry, the Poisonous Centipede
Harry the Poisonous Centipede's Big Adventure
I, Houdini
The Fairy Rebel
The Farthest Away Mountain

Stealing Stacey

Collins

An imprint of HarperCollins*Publishers*

First published in Great Britain by HarperCollins*Children's Books* 2004
HarperCollins*Children's Books* is an imprint of HarperCollins*Publishers* Ltd
77-85 Fulham Palace Road, Hammersmith, London W6 8JB

The HarperCollins website address is:

www.harpercollins.co.uk

1 3 5 7 9 8 6 4 2

ISBN 0 00 715922 6

Text copyright © Lynne Reid Banks 2004

Homestead illustration © Ian Warburton 1989

The author asserts the moral right to be identified as the author of this work.

Printed and bound in England by
Clays Ltd, St Ives plc

For Diane McCudden, who was the
inspiration for this book and the greatest
help in getting it right, and for Sarah,
who gave me the Wonngai stories.

Chapter One

Of course it would have to be the day the truant-cop brought me home, that this unbelievable woman turned up who was going to change my life.

Me and Loretta'd decided to bunk off after lunch. We had a great time... up to the point we were caught. First thing I wanted to do was change out of my rotten uniform. I'd brought a crop-top and we went to a café. Loretta marched straight through to the toilet with her head in the air, as if we were their best customers, and I changed. I had to keep my school skirt on, but I rolled the waistband down as far as I dared and stuffed my blazer and shirt into my school bag. Loretta didn't change. I guessed why. She gave my bare middle a pat and said, "Let's go."

So then we went and had our nails done – her sister's a

manicurist and she gave us two for the price of one when her manageress wasn't looking. Loretta paid. She's always got plenty of dosh. I had mine painted half white and half magenta, with squared-off points. Loretta had hers blue with silver stars stuck on each fingernail and moons on the thumbs. She bites hers so she couldn't do much about the sticking-out part – cos mine were longer she was really jealous.

Then we went to the covered market. There's a stall there that only sells lacy underwear. The woman who keeps the stall had nipped off to the loo and while she was gone Loretta nicked some pants and a matching bra. That was just for starters.

I didn't nick anything. From this point in time, a year later, I'm glad I didn't, but at the time – I have to tell the truth – it wasn't because I was dead honest, it was because I bottled it. I didn't know how she did it, she was so *quick* you couldn't even see her hands move. For the undies, she suddenly said, "Oh, look!" She pointed at something, and I looked where she pointed, and by the time I looked back she was moving away and the bra and pants were already stuffed up her school shirt, under her arm. (That was why she hadn't changed. You can't stuff much up a crop-top.) I didn't even know it till we got away from the stall and she showed me a tiny corner of the pants, yellowy-green and lacy. She was giggling like crazy. She showed them to me properly when we went back into the café. She got all her loot out of various hiding places, and laid it out on her knee under the table.

"Wicked," I said. But then I saw the pants were a size sixteen. "What d'you nick those for? You won't fit them."

"I'm not fussy," she said. "Turns me on, nicking things. I'll give 'em to my mum."

"Won't she ask where you got them?"

"Not her. Why should she? Pennies from heaven. I mean pants."

"Does she know you go on the rob?"

She shrugged. She'd got this round face, and while I'd been changing she'd been putting on lots of make up. She pulled funny faces all the time, too, and now she crossed her eyes and wobbled her head. Loretta thought everything was one big joke, but when I asked if she wasn't scared of getting caught she looked at me as if I was nuts, as if bad things could never happen to her.

Well, a bad thing happened to both of us that day, because we were just coming out of the café when the truant wagon draws up and a truant-cop gets out right in front of us.

"Afternoon, young ladies," he says, all polite, but stern with it. "Shouldn't you two be in school?"

I'm half up the nearest wall, straight off, don't know what to say, but Loretta's dead cool. She tosses her head and goes, "We had exams today and we finished early so we were allowed to go."

"Exams at the beginning of November? I don't think so!"

"They're special ones for high achievers," she says. "Extra." Honest, she's incredible.

"High achievers, eh?" he says. "Well, it's always nice to meet clever girls. We'll just make sure, shall we?" He looks at her blazer and straight off knows what school we're from by the badge, gets out his mobile and just clicks one button. He must have all the local school numbers in its memory. Of course I know right off the game's up, and so does Loretta, but while I'm stood there nearly wetting myself in panic she's leaning against a shop front, looking at her new silver-star nails. You'd've never thought she had all that nicked gear in her school bag.

By the time he'd found out that his suspicions were right – our school'd just put in the new computer program for spotting bunkers – it was too late to take us back to school, so he bundled us into his van (Loretta actually demanded to see his ID!) and took us home. When she got out of the van first, she gave me one of her funny looks and at the last moment, do you know what she did, she dumped her school bag on my lap and said, "Can you take this to your place? I'll come round and revise with you after I have my piano lesson." Piano lesson my bum – she just didn't want to risk being caught with the loot.

She nearly landed me in it as well, because the truant-cop soon spotted that I lived too far away for her to "come round" easily. He made some suspicious remark, gave me a funny look and then he looked at the school bag. I thought he was going to reach for it and I was terrified, but something distracted him and next thing I remember we were climbing the stone steps to Mum's and my flat.

"You don't have to come up with me," I muttered, but he came anyway of course. He would. He hadn't gone to Loretta's door, only mine. Story of my life with Loretta. She did all the villainy and I was the one who copped it.

"I need to have a word with your mum," he said.

Well, I wasn't too worried because I thought she'd probably be at work. She often does the afternoon shift at Safeways. I got my key out, but before I could open the door it was flung open from inside and there she was. She looked as if someone had given her an E or something, her eyes were bulging and her voice was all shrill.

"You'll never guess who's here!" she said loudly. "Not in a million years!" She was making her eye signals. When

11

Mum gets going with her eye signals you'd think she was going to have a fit.

Then she saw the truant-cop behind me and stopped dead.

"Who are you?" she asked.

"I'm the truant officer, madam," he said. "We found your daughter outside the market when she should have been at school. I don't know if this is the first time she's truanted, but I'm sure you understand that if she does it too often you may be held responsible."

Mum looked gobsmacked. She pulled me in through the door by the arm.

"She won't do it again," she said. "I'll see to that." But she said it very faintly, almost whispering. "Thank you." And she closed the door on him.

"You don't have to thank him, Mum," I said. "Big butt-in! We only took the afternoon off."

She put her finger to her lips – shhhh. Then I remembered what she'd said, before.

"What did you mean about someone being here?"

"I don't want you playing truant, Stace," she said in that same whisper. "Did you know mothers can go to prison if they let their kids bunk off?"

"Not the first time, Mum, only if you *never* make me go to school. So who's here?"

12

She was still whispering, her eyes rolling like some loony. "Someone I don't want you to shame me in front of," she said. "Your other nan."

I gawped at her. "What you mean, other nan?" I said like an idiot.

"Your other *grandma*."

My other grandma? Well, nobody has more than two. The nan I knew about was my mum's mum, so this one must be—

But that was impossible.

Now Mum was squeezing my arm tight and kind of wheeling me up to the mirror that hangs in our little lobby where we hang our coats. She was eye-signalling more madly than ever. I tried to read the signals. I'm quite good at it – I should be, after fourteen years' practice. It was something like, *I hadn't a clue she was coming... she's in the living room... I nearly died... the place is such a tip... so are you... for God's sake do something about it before you go in there!*

No, I'm not pretending to be that good. Her hands were signalling, too. They were fussing about all over me. Trying to pull my top down to cover my middle. Unrolling my skirt and pulling it up (and down). Reaching into her handbag, fetching out a grotty little comb and thrusting it at me, talking in that loud voice all the time.

"Think of it, Stacey, all the way from *Australia*! Of course she wrote to warn us but she forgot to put enough stamps on it – it must still be on a boat somewhere! Never MIND, it's just so great to *see* her, aren't you excited that she's come to see us, I am!" *I know, I know – it's terrible – but PLEASE remember your manners!* signalled her eyes. They were now crossing and rolling so much I was afraid they'd fall out.

I scraped the comb over my hair, just to shut her up (I'd done my hair that morning with *Just Out Of Bed: Keep That Messed-up Look All Day* wax) and went into the living room. I admit I was curious. Who wouldn't be? Because this was my dad's mum. Why would she come to see us from Australia, when Dad never did from Greville Drive, two miles away? Didn't she know he'd scarpered?

In the doorway, I stopped dead. A kind of *vision* was sitting there on our sofa.

She had short curly hair, very blue-rinsed and just-been-done, and a two-piece suit with a short skirt and high-heeled shoes to match. Underneath her jacket she wore a fancy spotted blouse with ruffles and a bow at the neck. All of it was in shades of mauve and purple. And lots and lots of make-up. The eye make-up was purple, too. And she was smiling a big smile with bright white (false?) teeth.

"Blossom, come to Grandma!" she said in an Aussie accent that'd put *Neighbours* to shame, and reached for me.

Mum gave me a push from behind. I sort of fell forward into this stranger's arms. She smelt as if she'd emptied a bottle of Eau de Pong over herself. That, and spearmint, from the gum she was chewing. The gum-chewing didn't go with any other thing about her.

After she'd hugged and kissed me she pulled me down on the sofa beside her.

"You ravishing little angel!" she cried. "Aren't you pretty, you little wavy blondie, you! With those *blue* eyes! You get those from me!" She batted her mascaraed eyelashes. She had blue eyes, just like my dad. "And I *love* your *nails*! If only mine were long, I'd have 'em done just like yours! Oh, why did I wait this long to meet you? You and me are just going to be the pals of the *millennium*!" She had one arm round my neck and she was holding my head on her shoulder. I thought my head would come off, but I managed to straighten up before it did.

"You two have just the cosiest little nest here!" the vision was saying, looking round our hovel. I saw her glancing at some of the photos. There were still ones of Dad and of him and Mum together on their wedding day, and of the three of us, all of which I'd have chucked in the bin the day he bombed off. In fact I did, but Mum fished them out, and she was crying so much I hadn't the heart to chuck them again. "Little nest" was about right. With three of us

15

in the living room, it felt like three cuckoos were squashed into a sparrow's nest.

Mum looks a bit like a sparrow. I read that sparrows, which used to be the British birds we had the most of, are dying out for some reason, pollution maybe, and no wonder – you can hardly breathe where we live. Now Mum looked as if she might be the last of them. She has these round bright eyes, and she's soft and small with little pecky movements. She wasn't actually fluttering and twittering, but I knew she was, inside.

"D'you want a cup of tea, Mrs, er—" She stopped. Her face turned red. I heard myself say, a bit impatiently I admit, "Denton, Mum, it must be." Of course this nan must have the same name as us, my dad's name.

But she said, "Oh, call me Glendine, lovies, everyone does! We can't have two Mrs Dentons, can we? Too confusing! Besides," she added, "I don't suppose you want to be reminded of a certain Mr Run-Rabbit-Run."

I couldn't believe it. Dad was this woman's *son*. I kept staring at her, trying to connect her to Dad. Apart from the eyes, she didn't look anything like him. And she was slagging him off. It was weird.

Grandma said, "Did I hear the word 'tea'? Because I'd kill for some." And she got up off the sofa. God, she was tall! That *was* like Dad. Her blue rinse nearly bumped the

16

ceiling. Then she said, "But first I need a sweet pea." I must've looked blank because she laughed. "Point me at the dunny, darling, I'm busting." When I *still* looked blank, she said, "The la. The loo. The potty-house. The *toilet!*" I don't know why I was so embarrassed. Everyone has to go. It was just that my other nan would never mention toilets or anything else she calls "vulgar". When she has to go, she says, "I'm off to the excuse-me."

It turned out the vision preferred the kitchen, where we normally eat, to the living room. But she looked all wrong in there. Like a tropical bush in a window box.

She sat perched on a high stool at the counter, with her legs crossed. She had nice legs for an old woman, I'll say that, and she liked showing them off and all.

There was no problem about keeping the conversation going. She just couldn't stop gassing. She said the long flight from Australia had nearly killed her.

"I simply have to stretch out, petals," she said. "If I can't stretch my poor old legs, they get cramp." She stuck them straight out in front of her and nearly fell off the stool. "Ooops! No, but I'm serious. I was in agony! In the night when the crew turned the lights off and went behind their curtains, Glendine went on the prowl. I found a lovely little cave behind the last row of seats. So I

17

went and got my rug and my tiny cushion and I just laid down—"

"You lay on the floor?" gasped Mum. She was staring at her as if she'd come out of a flying saucer.

"Why not? It was quite comfy, I got a lovely kip. But of course my feet stuck out, and in the morning, a steward tripped over them! Just about broke me bloody ankle. You'd think he'd apologise, but not a bit of it – he was *livid*. 'Madam,' he said, 'lying on the floor of the aircraft is strictly against regulations, you will have to return to your seat!' I sat up and gave him my biggest smile. I said, 'Of course, pet, no worries.' And I gave him my hand, to pull me up, very graciously, just like the Queen. I got back to my seat in nice time for brekky. And then, would you believe? They made a special announcement to the *whole plane* that it was forbidden to lay down on the floor! I think they had to make a new regulation, just for Glendine!"

Me and Mum laughed. I thought, *I bet everywhere you go, they have to make up new regulations just for you.* I didn't know how right I was.

We were halfway through tea (she still hadn't stopped talking) when I started thinking about where she was going to stay.

Surely not with us? We only have two bedrooms. I had another thought. Where was her luggage? Of course! It must be at her hotel. Phew.

After tea I excused myself and went to my room. When I opened the door, I got a mega shock. I saw where her luggage was, all right.

I counted the pieces. There were four and a half. They all matched – bright orange with yellow sunflowers all over them – and went from a small box-thing on a shoulder strap, to a trunk. You certainly couldn't miss them coming around on the airport carousel. You couldn't miss them in my room, either. In fact I could hardly get in for them.

I suddenly felt desperate. Not only was she planning to stay – she must be planning to stay for ever.

Just then Mum came in behind me. She shut the door. We were squeezed together behind the trunk. She said, in a very soft voice, "Yes. I'm sorry, Stace."

I just stared at her. Then I whispered, "How did all this stuff get here?"

"She came from the airport in two taxis. The taxi-men carried it up. She tipped them a tenner each!"

"She must be rotten with dosh. Why doesn't she go to a hotel?"

"She said she wants to be with us."

"Can't she see we've got *no room*?"

19

"I – I'm afraid I said you wouldn't mind moving in with me."

I couldn't speak for a moment. For horror.

"But I'll have to sleep in your bed!" I wailed.

"Shhh! We must be nice to her."

I didn't feel like shushing. "*Why?*"

"I don't know really," said Mum. "I just know we must."

That was so like Mum. You probably think she was thinking that this person was rich and we ought to suck up to her, maybe, but that wasn't it. Mum doesn't know *why* anything. She just does things. It's like she acts on instinct. I bet if someone had asked her why she was marrying my dad, she'd have said, in that same helpless voice, "I don't know exactly. I just know I must."

Come to that, I bet Nan did ask her. Nan stayed married to my grandad for forty-two years and she'd be married to him still if he hadn't gone and died. *She'd* never have married a no-hoper like Dad. Fancy watching your kid do something that stupid and not be able to talk her out of it. That's why I'd decided I was never going to get married. Even if I'd liked boys, which naturally, considering what a bunch of duck-brained wussy creeps they are, I did *not*, I wouldn't let myself get tied up to someone who might run out on me and leave me penniless and probably up the duff. (Of course Mum's too old to be up the duff. Which is one good thing at least.)

Anyhow, there it was. I kicked up a terrible fuss (but quietly – even I didn't want the vision to hear) but in the end I had to move out of my room. I was so upset I was crying. We carried my clothes and the rest of my clobber into Mum's room. She's got the double bed from when Dad was around. At least she had a washbasin in the room. I thought, *Good, cos I bet when "Glen-deen" – of all the stupid names – gets in the bathroom, she puts down roots.* This was going to be a nightmare.

I started to sink down on the bed. Mum pulled me up before I touched. "No, you don't. Back you go and talk to her. I'll arrange your stuff."

"Mum! I won't know where anything is!"

"I'm going to give you half of all my space. Even my dressing-table top."

"Big deal!"

"Yes, it is. Now go and talk to your grandmother."

"What am I supposed to call her? I'm not calling her Nan, I've got a nan already!"

"Call her Grandma then."

I went slowly back into the kitchen. Grandma (ugh! Who says "Grandma"?) was washing the tea things at the sink. I took over – she was a guest after all.

She took off Dad's stripy apron. "Did my wild Australian boy leave this?" she said, dangling it. "I bet that's all he

21

did leave! I never saw the domestic side of him, I must say! When did he nick off, the little mongrel?"

I was shocked *rigid*. She was his mum, after all. Mums are supposed to be on their kids' side. "Two years ago," I mumbled.

That shook her.

"Two years… And I never knew! Any excuses?"

"No. Him and Mum had a last row. He slammed out and that was it."

"You don't know where he is?"

"Yeah, we do. Living with his girlfriend in Greville Drive."

"Where's Greville Drive?"

"Ten minutes' bus ride from here."

"So how come he sent me a postcard from Thailand?"

I nearly dropped a mug. Thailand? My mouth went all dry.

Grandma went on, "It just about made me throw up from shame."

I said, "Please – uh – Grandma – Glendine, don't tell Mum. Greville Drive was bad enough."

"I bet!" she said. "When I saw that postcard I thought, sounds like he's living it up. That's when I decided to pack up and come over and see how you fellas were getting on." *Well, we're not*, I thought. *We're in the crap. We've got no* money, Mum's working her socks off at the checkout and everything's horrible. What can you do about it?

Then I remembered those ten-quid tips. And the posh luggage. And the way she dressed. I couldn't help it – I thought, *She's really rich.* I wondered why Dad never mentioned that. He never had any readies. Whenever he *had* a job, we didn't see much money from it. Most of it went on booze. And dope, if you ask me. We didn't know that for sure, and he always flat denied it, but there's a difference between the way people get when they're pissed and when they're stoned.

"How do you think he managed to go to Thailand?" Grandma was asking.

After a bit, I said, "I think his girlfriend had some money."

My mum had called her a little slapper, among other things I won't repeat. But Greville Drive is quite posh. Compared to our road, anyway. It was houses, not flats. She most likely put up the cash. She was probably in Phoo-kuk or whatever the place is called with him right this minute, lying on a beach wearing three triangles of lace tied on with string, under a bunch of palm trees. Thinking of this made *me* want to throw up. Not from shame, though. From rage. Whatever problems I have with my mum, she doesn't deserve to be treated like that.

Chapter Two

Grandma Glendine settled in with us.

I hated her being there, but not because of her so much. It was because I had to share Mum's room. And Mum not only smokes – she snores.

"Mum! Roll over!" I'd shout when her snores were driving me wild. The most infuriating thing was that Mum simply refused to believe that she snored.

"It's lies, I don't! Dad would've told me."

"Probably too stoned to notice." I shouldn't have said that. She just turned her back and her shoulders started to shake. I knew she was still crazy for him.

Somehow Gran – I'd decided to call her just Gran – arranged her things in my room. She used all that luggage as extra furniture. The trunk turned into a table. Gran wrote loads of postcards on it, all touristy pictures of London, beefeaters at the Tower, guards at Buckingham Palace, that kind of thing. Even some of Princess Diana. She said a funny thing about her, that I should have taken more notice of at the time, but I didn't.

"I remember exactly where I was when I heard she'd died. I was skinning a kangaroo."

I don't know *why* I didn't pick up on that. I just thought it was a joke or something. I sometimes think I'm not very bright.

The other suitcases were piled up and she stood things on them. She'd brought lots of interesting things with her.

There were postcards of pictures all painted in dots. I couldn't make them out until she explained them. They were painted by Australian natives and were all in code. A fire was a bunch of red dots, for instance, and white dotted lines were trips their ancestors made in something called the Dreamtime, across the outback. That's the middle of Australia where it's all desert. And there were special kinds of dots for animals or their footprints, or curvy coloured lines for snake tracks. The animals were wonderful weird kinds. I loved those postcards and Gran gave me some to stick up on my side of Mum's dressing-table mirror.

Then there were some wooden animals with burn marks on them. Big lizardy things called goannas, and snakes (I wouldn't even touch those. God how I hated snakes, not that I'd ever seen a live one). She had miniature wooden things like long bowls and something called a throwing stick, for spears, she said. She gave me a boomerang, only where would I have space to try throwing it? She showed me a picture of a didgeridoo, a musical instrument, which is a long, thick pipe. It gets hollowed out by termites, and it's so heavy you have to rest the far end, the end away from your mouth, on the ground. She told me women aren't allowed to play it because it's symbolic, you can guess what of!

She showed off her clothes. They were sort of naff in a way, but rich-naff, not like Mum's shell suit that I told her not to buy at the Oxfam shop (but of course she did). It's a sort of metal-pink. I die every time she goes out in it.

Gran took us out. Not on week nights, she was very hot on me getting to bed early so I wouldn't be tired at school, but on Fridays and Saturdays. She took us for meals out, and not at the local dumps, either, except once we took her to one of the African cafés for the experience. I took her around the market a couple of times, she said she loved it, which was quite something, because it can be fun in the summer, but it's pretty dismal in the rain. Mainly though, she wanted to treat us. Once we went to a Holiday Inn right up West and had a really swish meal with proper waiters. That was the night she took us to see the show at the Hippodrome. It was amazing. I'd never seen a live act before. She took us to loads of good movies too. We took taxis and minicabs everywhere, she wouldn't ride the buses or trains.

She talked. How she talked! And she wanted me to talk, too. When I came home from school she asked me to tell her my whole day. I was used to slumping in front of the telly after school to chill out. Now I had to *articulate*. She soon spotted I hated school. She never mentioned the truant-cop, but I think she'd heard, or maybe Mum had ratted on me.

"It's really bad not to like school, sweetie," she said. (By now I'd lost count of all her pet names for me.) "You have to get your priorities right. School's a top priority at your age."

"It's so boring."

"It's up to teachers to make learning fun."

"Tell that to ours," I said.

"Kids have to make an effort too," she said. She fixed me with her eyes. She wasn't reproaching me exactly, more sort of measuring me. "Isn't there any lesson you like?"

I didn't answer at once. I didn't want to tell her I quite liked English, for some reason. I fancied myself as an anti-school rebel, like Loretta. But she kept her eyes fixed on me, so in the end I muttered that computer studies weren't bad.

27

Gran brightened up. "Oh, good that you like computers! I'm surprised you don't have one at home."

I gave Mum a look. I'd *begged*, just about on my knees, for a home computer. I'd told her, like one million times, that my teacher said that was one reason why I wasn't keeping up, cos I didn't have a PC. I was pretty well the only one in my class that didn't. (Well, that was what I told Mum anyway.)

"Now don't start, Stace, you don't need a computer!" Mum snapped at me. "It's up to the school to make you keep up, without telling me I ought to spend hundreds of pounds we haven't got."

"Of course she needs one," said Gran. "A good one, with a colour printer and a scanner and all the bits. Christmas is coming, isn't that right, cherry pie?" and she winked at me.

"Glendine! Don't even think about it, *please*!" said Mum. "I couldn't accept it."

"Rubbish! Why not?"

"Because... I don't know why not. I just feel I couldn't." Typical Mum. Gran just smiled her big white smile. (Her teeth weren't false. I knew because Nan's were and I could tell the difference, close to.) I felt my heart sort of bob up and down. I knew I'd get a computer for Christmas and there wasn't a thing Mum could do about it.

I had it all worked out by the beginning of December. Where I'd set it up would be in the living room. I'd surf the net and send e-mails and join chat rooms and play computer games. I might even use it for a bit of schoolwork.

But then in the end I didn't get a computer at all. Because Gran got a better idea.

She told me it was a secret.

"Not a word to Mum yet! I'm going to kidnap you."

"Go on, Gran. You're just having me on, right?"

"I'm serious. I couldn't be more serious if I tried."

I couldn't take it in at first. It was too amazing. She wanted to take me to Australia for the Christmas holiday!

I was, like, *ecstatic*. The more she told me about Australia, the more I wanted to see it. She made it sound so exciting. She had a wonderful book with coloured photos in. Everything looked so *different* from boring old England.

It seemed like the sun shone all the time, there was tons of swimming and sports, and lots of wildlife. I'm really into wildlife, on the telly, that is. There's not much of it in south London – unless you count birds. And I saw an urban fox once. But foxes and pigeons don't stack up against dingoes and koalas and wallabies and wombats and duck-billed platypuses. That's aside from kangaroos, which have been my favourite animal since I had a Kanga and Roo toy when I was little. The snakes put me off a bit, but I tried not to think about them. Or the crocodiles. We've got no dangerous animals at all in Britain, unless you count the

Loch Ness Monster and the Beast of Bodmin Moor, which nobody really believes in. About our most dangerous thing apart from Rottweilers is mosquitoes. (OK, adders. But in London? Get real.)

But what I wanted to see most was the outback, because I'd seen videos of *Priscilla, Queen of the Desert* and *Crocodile Dundee*. But it was because of Gran's things, too, what she called her Aboriginal artefacts. I wanted to meet some of those people.

"There are big mobs of Wonngais where I come from," she said carelessly. "I'll introduce you."

I was just so scared Mum wouldn't let me go.

"Don't you worry about that! You leave your mum to me."

But before she could tackle Mum, something really radical happened.

When I think back to it now, I remember what a good day we'd had, the day before. First off, we'd had a row, because I'd been to Loretta's, supposedly just for a sleepover, and of course we weren't supposed to go anywhere, but we did. We sneaked out to a party and danced and, yes, we did drink a few alcopops, actually more than a few, but it wouldn't have mattered – I mean we didn't get legless or anything, we were just enjoying ourselves. But by the lousiest luck on earth, the son of a friend of Mum's was there (the others were mostly older than us) and he must've ratted on me. When I got home the next morning, which was Saturday and Mum's day off from the checkout, Mum was waiting for me. She was practically jumping up and down. It was just lucky for me Gran was there or I would've really copped it. Even as it was, Mum dragged me off to our room and had a hissy-fit and I had one back, but even the hissing was kind of muffled because we knew Gran was listening.

When I can't yell back at Mum it all sort of turns inwards – I felt all screwed up inside and I just lay on the bed crying and feeling like it was the end of the world. Of course Loretta wasn't going to cop it, was she. Just me. And Mum'd grounded me for two weeks, just when there were Christmas parties and other things coming up.

Then I heard Gran's and Mum's voices and I tried to listen, but all I could tell was that Gran was trying to calm Mum down. After a bit, Mum crept back into our room and sat down on the bed and said, in that little-girl way she has, "Gran's on your side. She says it was only a bit of fun and I'm too hard on you. She says I should do more things with you and then you wouldn't want to get away from me all the time and be rebellious." (Can you imagine? She is so *transparent*. But it's sort of sweet in a way, she just can't play the heavy-mother game for long, it isn't in her nature.)

I sniffed and blew my nose and said, "Like what things?" I mean, what could she possibly have in mind that was interesting? But your parents can surprise you, just sometimes.

"How would you like to get your bellybutton pierced?"

I sat up on the bed and stared at her, eyes boggling.

"*What?*"

She said it again, and then she said something even more unexpected.

"I've always wanted a bellybutton ring. We could do it together."

Well, of course, that did it. Mother and daughter bellybutton rings. I ask you. Who could hold out against that? Because I knew as sure as eggs is eggs (as Nan says) that having any part of her pierced was the last thing on earth Mum had ever dreamt of, I mean otherwise she wouldn't still be wearing clip-on earrings and always losing them.

So off we went that same day and had our bellybuttons pierced together at that place on the high street. She went absolutely white as a ghost when it was her turn and I suddenly felt I loved her. You know when you sort of love someone all the time, in the background, with rows and sulks and stuff going on in the foreground, you forget to really *feel* it, and then unexpectedly you do feel it and it nearly knocks you down. I gave her a big hug and said, "You don't have to do it if you don't want to, Mum," but she said she did want to and in she went to the torture chamber, brave as a lion, and had it done. And now we both had a sort of secret together because she said she'd never show hers, it would just be for me to know about. (She went all quiet for a bit after she said it, and I knew she was thinking "Except Dad if he ever comes back." But I was pretty sure he never would, and she knew that, so she didn't say it aloud. She hates me telling her to get real.)

Afterwards she took me out for a pizza and it was a good laugh. We talked, mainly about our sore bellybuttons it's true, but a bit about other things, and I told her all about the party and I heard myself promise never to go to one again where there was alcohol, until she told me I could. (To be honest, it was a bit scary, practically everyone there was older than us and there were some dodgy types among the boys – I mean apart from that rotten sneak. One of them touched my tummy. I didn't tell Mum that of course.)

In the afternoon we met Gran and she took us to a movie, her choice. She wanted us to see an Australian film called *Rabbit-Proof Fence*. It was really wonderful, all about two Aborigine sisters, young kids, who run away from this horrible school and walk hundreds of miles through a desert to get home. It was really sad, especially at the end when you saw these women who were the real girls, grown old. We all cried, even Gran, who'd seen it before.

So that was our good day.

Then it happened.

I heard the phone ringing in the middle of the night, and felt Mum get out of our bed. Then I went back to sleep. In the morning, she was gone. Gone! Just like that! I couldn't believe it, but I had to after I found the note on my side of the dressing table.

"Stacey, I'm sorry, I have to go. Dad's in trouble. Gran'll look after you. I'll be back soon, I hope. Love, Mum."

She'd taken some of her things. I rushed into my bedroom that was Gran's now. I didn't even knock. I woke her up and showed her the note. I was in a state, all shocked and crying.

Gran sat up in bed. She had a shiny, bare night-face. She read the note. "Oh the precious little idiot," she said. "Wouldn't I like to give her curry!"

"Curry!"

"That's Australian for a hot telling-off." Then she hugged me tight. "Don't you cry, sweet-face. Grandma Glendine's here. She'll take care of you."

I pulled away. "But where's she gone? She couldn't go to Thailand, she hasn't got a passport!"

"Let's try Greville Drive, it's closer."

34

"You mean Dad's come back?"

"I wouldn't wonder, if he's phoned her to say he's in trouble."

It was Sunday, luckily. Gran told me to go and put the kettle on while she got dressed. She had her tea and then she called a minicab and we drove round to Greville Drive. I knew it was number six because Mum went there once just to look at the place. She'd have gone more times if I hadn't stopped her. It was like she was addicted, just to seeing where he lived... *sick*! With Gran, I stayed in the cab. I didn't want to see Dad, just Mum. I wanted to see her so badly, it was like there wasn't anything else that mattered. I was sort of sniffing-crying, trying to hold it back. Gran marched up the path and rang the bell. She soon came marching back.

"No good. It's some new people. He hasn't been back there. They could be anywhere. I can't believe your mum. What a prize little nitwit. After the way he treated her, he only has to crook his little finger and she goes running back! And to God knows what sort of a mess." She slammed the car door and told the driver to take us home. It was like sitting in a minicab next to a volcano. I could almost see the steam coming out of her blue rinse.

* * *

35

So me and Gran turned into flatmates.

She cooked sometimes, but she liked it better when I did. She sat in the kitchen on a high stool, chewed her gum, and watched me. I tried out some of the stuff I'd seen on the TV cooking programmes. Mum'd never let me, she said I used too many pots and then left her to wash them up. (She had a point. I hate washing up. I'd almost rather have a dishwasher than a computer.) Gran thought I was brilliant. Every time I put in a couple of grinds of pepper or beat up some eggs, she acted as if I was Jamie Oliver. This was nice, but I was missing Mum like crazy. I got more and more upset that she didn't phone. Love is really weird. When she was there, she drove me mad. Now I'd lie in our bed wishing she was snoring beside me, or puffing on a fag, though I always used to shout at her that she'd set the bed on fire.

"She'll be back, dolly-face, and most likely with a flea in her ear," Gran said. "Serve her right. Women shouldn't be doormats. But we'll have to give her loads of TLC." (That's Tender Loving Care, in case you don't know.)

At last Mum phoned. She'd been gone three days and fifteen hours.

"Mum!" I screamed down the phone. "Where are you? Are you coming home?"

"No, Stace, I can't. I'm just ringing to see that you're all right."

"Well I'm not! How could I be, without you?"

"You're actually missing me?" she said, in a really surprised voice.

"Of course I am!" I yelled.

"Why? What do you miss?"

I felt furious and at the same time, lousy. She was as good as saying I'd never appreciated her, never let her know I loved her. "Everything," I said. "Even your snoring. Please come home."

There was a long silence and then she said, in a muffled sort of voice, "Stace, listen. Don't tell Glendine this – she is still there?"

"Yes."

"Oh, good. Well, don't tell her, but Dad's… he's sort of on the run."

"Mum! What's he done?"

"I can't tell you. But he's hiding out and I have to stand by him and help him. He's got no one else."

"What about the slapper?"

"She's gone."

"Did you – did you know they went to Thailand?"

"Yes. That was where he… got into trouble. Where *she* got him into trouble. He managed to pinch his ticket back from her before she left him, and fly home, but the police there put the ones here on to him. Now, don't think badly of him, Stace—"

"Oh, no, I wouldn't do that!" I said, really sarky. I was feeling sick and scared. What could he have done? It had to be something to do with drugs. I'd heard plenty about men luring women into carrying drugs for them, but never the other way round. I hated to feel Dad was weak, that she'd used him.

"It wasn't his fault," Mum almost shouted, in a very strong voice. "It was her, that's who it was, and then when she'd landed him in it, she ran out on him when he needed her most, the rotten little tramp. I knew she was no good, those tarted-up middle-class ones with their snooty voices are the worst! Stacey, I just want to ask you, can you manage for a bit longer till I sort things out for Dad? I wouldn't ask, but this is a real emergency."

All my helpless, angry thoughts suddenly came together to form one word. One answer.

Australia. On the other side of the world. An escape from everything: this lousy little flat; school; the miserable weather we were having, all muggy or else dark and pissing down with rain all the time; Christmas on our own with no money; Dad in a mess, Mum stuck with him… No. None of it was my fault. I didn't have to put up with it or face it. I could get away from all of it. Australia!

I knew I should tell her. I knew it. But I thought she'd say I couldn't go.

"I'll be all right, Mum," I said. And I even heard myself add, "Give Dad my love." But I didn't mean it. Not really. I was ready to clobber him for taking Mum away from me.

I didn't tell Gran about the call.

That same day, she asked, sort of carelessly, "When does school break up?"

"On the seventeenth."

"Oh, right."

When I came home from school on the last day of term, I found the flat in, like, *chaos*. I thought at first we'd been done over. Then I looked closer and saw the suitcases. Her sunflower ones, open. One of them was full of summer clothes. Not her size. Mine.

I picked up a green and purple bikini and dropped it again. "Gran! What's going on?" I shouted.

She popped out of her (my) room. She sort of sang, "Glen-dine's been shop-ping!"

"I can see! What's it all for?"

"It's all for you, cookie. I hope you like it. I'd have taken you to help choose, but we're leaving tomorrow, there was no time."

"Leaving? Where are we going?" But I knew. And suddenly it was real. She was kidnapping me, just as she'd promised!

"We're flying to Perth, love," she said. "Not Perth, Scotland. Perth, Australia."

"What? But we can't! Don't I need a passport?"

"You've got one, ducky!" she said, triumphant. She held up a new red passport. I took it from her and looked at it. There was a picture of me that we'd had taken in a booth one day when I was out with her, she'd said she wanted it for a souvenir.

It struck me a lot later that she must've been planning this for a long time. She'd have needed Mum's signature on the form, so she must've forged it. But I never thought of any of it. Not at the time. I was too upset about Mum and Dad, and now there was something really exciting going to happen to make up for it.

Chapter Three

I had my doubts – give me that much. That night while Gran was having one of her endless baths – she'd imported a big bottle of bubble bath, which I could hear her frothing up with her hands till it must've looked like she was lying in a huge milkshake – I phoned Nan and told her I was going to Australia with my other grandmother.

Nan was already in a state about Mum bombing off. She'd been round a few times to see I was all right. She didn't like Glendine, I could tell. She always turned her head away, as if Gran was too bright for her eyes. Now Nan said, in her pursed-up-lips voice, "I don't think it's right, her carrying you off like that without so much as a by-your-leave."

"How can we ask Mum, when she's gone off?"

"She'll be back. Then what's she going to say?"

"I'm leaving her a note. And you can explain. Besides, I'll be back before school starts. Nan, I want to go!"

Nan fussed and carried on. She didn't want me to go, but I remembered Mum'd said she was jealous of Gran, because of her throwing her dosh around and giving us treats. In the end I just said, "Well I'm going. I'll send you a postcard with a kangaroo on it, bye." That was that, because I put down the phone. Yeah, rude. But if you don't bring Nan's phone calls to an end she can witter on at you for hours.

What bothered me much more, after I'd hung up, was that I hadn't told her I'd heard from Mum. I just left her to worry. But wouldn't she have worried even more if I'd told her about Dad being in trouble with the law?

I'd never flown before. It was a long flight but I didn't care. I loved it. I wasn't even impatient, because Gran told me her self-hypnosis technique for long flights.

"You settle down and put your seat belt on, and you think, 'Nothing to do but sit here and read magazines and watch movies and eat and drink and sleep and look forward to Australia!'" I did that and it worked. I suppose I'm naturally lazy, like my teacher says (what she actually said was, I was *seriously talented* at laziness), because doing nothing for thirteen and a half hours didn't bother me a bit.

I wanted to see if Gran would sleep on the floor again, but she didn't. She got very uncomfortable though. She sighed and groaned and wriggled and said her legs were killing her. I felt really sorry for her with her long legs all cramped up, or out in the aisle where people kept kicking them, but not so much when she fell asleep sprawled all over me.

We landed in Singapore and had a wonderful Chinese meal in the airport. I wanted to go into the town (we had to wait three hours) but Gran said, "We're not allowed, and anyway you wouldn't like it. It's the opposite of London, it's the cleanest city on earth, and if you drop so much as a sweet wrapper they put you in jail and flog you." Then we flew on to Perth.

I was already in my new clothes. Gran had different taste for me than for her. She'd bought me really cool gear. I was surprised about one thing – it was all casual stuff. She'd said we were going to stay at a hotel, and I supposed that meant dressing up (it didn't, as it turned out), so what did I need two pairs of combat pants and three pairs of army-looking shorts for? Not to mention all those sleeveless tops.

When we got to Perth I liked it straight away. It was lovely and clean, even without jail and flogging. You could taste the air. The sea was blue and the weather was hot – there were loads of parks and flowers, and gumtrees like in the movies about Australia, that had smooth trunks all patchy green and white, and leaves that smelt like rubbing oil. Some beautiful coloured parrot-things were flying in them.

We checked into a fantastic hotel. I'd never seen anything like it. It was *so grand*. I had my own room and beautiful bathroom. Gran had the room next door. We unpacked a bit and then had lunch in a big dining room with a buffet. The food! It was unbelievable. Everything you could ever think of to eat, all laid out on silver dishes. Things like baby lobsters. Oysters. Chicken. Duck. Pink roast beef. A zillion salads and hot dishes, and mountains of fruit and cheeses, half of which I'd never seen in my life. There were about ten different kinds of fish. The desserts were like a dream, coloured jellies and flans and creamy cakes and fruit salads like a mass of jewels, and lots more. You helped yourself. You could choose anything you liked, as much as you liked, and come back for more. I thought I'd died and gone to heaven. I think if we'd stayed there for long I would have died, from overeating.

Gran ate oysters till I lost count. I tried one. Yuck! It was like solid snot. She laughed when I said that. She was laughing a lot. Then, just as I was eating my third pudding, something went clunk in my head and I nearly fell asleep right into the whipped cream. Gran saw my eyes closing.

"You're jet-lagged," she said. "Come on, sweetness. Bed for you."

In my room I dropped on to the big double bed. I felt Gran pulling my shoes off. That was all I knew. When I woke up it was dark. I lay awake looking out of the window at the stars. They were so big and clear! After a bit, I fell back to sleep. I felt so happy. England and school were just nowhere. As for Mum and Dad… I pushed them out of my mind. I didn't want anything to get in the way of having a wonderful time.

Next day everything was a bit crazy. We had breakfast at lunch time, then went for a drive in a cab round the city to see the rich people's big houses. Then we had a swim in the wonderful blue sea. The beach was great. There were a lot of really *fit* tanned boys and some of them looked at me in my new bikini, but then they looked at Gran and kept away. But I felt really shy and embarrassed and wished I had a more cover-up cossie. Having a figure is only nice when you're showing it off to other girls – that's what I thought, I didn't like those boys eyeing me up and down.

We went out for dinner to a posh restaurant. It was in a tower that revolved while you ate – you could look at the lights coming on, and the stars shining on the river. They served cooked kangaroo, which Gran ate, but I wouldn't – I thought it was awful, like eating a horse or a dog. I had steak. I suppose that's just as bad, really. I fell asleep in the middle. I was really dopey. Gran said it was OK, she was like it herself. She said everyone gets jet lag and that I'd be better in a day or two.

She was right. The next day I felt great. She said tomorrow we were going travelling and I was going to see the outback, like I'd wanted. Of course I thought it would be some kind of day trip. I was so excited. I was loving every minute. I thought Gran was the greatest. She kept hugging and kissing me. She always had, but now I hugged her back. I felt I really loved her, I was just so grateful.

That evening Gran told me she had things to do in the morning, and that I was to pack and meet her in the lobby. "I'm ordering room service to bring you a lovely brekky in your room, then just come on down at ten. Don't you try to stagger down with your bags, precious," she said. "I'll send a bellboy. See ya!" I thought she had a funny smile, as if she had a surprise for me. Boy, did she.

When I came out of the lift next morning, I looked all round this vast lobby, but I couldn't see her. There was a tall man in a big-brimmed leather hat standing at the reception desk. My eyes went right past, still looking for Gran. Suddenly the tall man turned round. I got a real shock.

It wasn't a man, it was her! But even facing, I hardly recognised her. She'd changed her clothes. Her clothes? She'd changed everything. She was wearing combat trousers, a khaki shirt, and cowboy boots. She looked completely different. Even her blue hair was covered with the leather hat. She looked like Crocodile Dundee.

I came up to her slowly. "Gran, is it you? What have you done to yourself?"

She laughed, a big boomy laugh. "Well, sugar-puff, we're off to the bush! You don't expect me to doll myself up in town clothes for that, do you? Didn't I tell you there are two of me, a town person and a bushie? This is your bush Glendine!"

While we'd been in Perth we'd driven around in taxis. Now we went outside and waiting at the front of the hotel was one of those truck-things with an open back. Her luggage was piled in that, with a whole lot of other stuff. I thought I saw a sort of iron bed! The bellboy came along with my luggage and put it in with the rest, and helped Gran pull a piece of canvas over everything and tie it down. Gran said, "How d'you like my ute?"

"Ute?"

"Utility. That's what we call 'em."

"Did you say it's yours?"

"Sure. I've had it in a garage while I've been in London. They brought it to me this morning and I've been off to do a bit of shopping."

I looked at it. It was about the last kind of vehicle I'd've expected her to drive. To begin with I was surprised the doorman let her stand it outside the hotel, it was so rusty and old. It looked as if it might drop to pieces any minute and have to be dragged away.

There was a big metal bar in front.

"That's a roo bar," said Gran.

"Rhubarb?"

"No! Roo bar! It's so if you hit a roo – kangaroo – he doesn't damage the car. Hitting a roo can cause an awful dent to your ute."

I said, "Oh, please, don't hit one, Gran!"

She laughed and said, "They'd better keep out of my way then."

I soon saw what she meant.

We climbed up into the cabin. The seat covers were so worn the stuffing was coming out. It was a mess inside – big bottles of water everywhere and dangly things in the windows, and rubbish on the floor. I said, "What would they think of this in Singapore?"

Gran let out a kind of whoop of laughter. "They'd beat me to death!" She sounded happier than I'd ever heard her.

Then she just took off.

I've never seen anyone drive so fast. Even going through the town, I had to hang on tight. I was breath-stopped and it was only through good luck we weren't cop-stopped. When we got out on the country roads she zoomed along like someone lit her fuse.

"Gran, slow down!" I yelled.

"No fear, lovie! We've got a long way to go!"

Luckily after a bit we got on to a road with almost no traffic. I say "luckily" – it wasn't really, because then she went faster than ever.

At first there was forest on each side that seemed to go on for ever, but after that was even more for ever with what looked like sheep and wheat farms. It was endless, endless driving. I got sort of hypnotised by the long, dead straight road. Passing another vehicle was an event. There were a few enormous, humungous trucks with two or three containers attached. Gran called them road trains. But there wasn't much else on the road at all.

Then it changed. On either side were low banks of bright red earth, and trees and bushes, sort of greyish-green, not like English ones. It just went on and on, mile after mile the same. I said to Gran, "Is this it – the bush?"

"Well, you know what they say! The bush is always 50 k on from wherever you are! But I'd call this the beginning of it."

I said, "I thought it would be more, like, desert."

"This is a sort of desert. It's very dry. But it's full of life. Snakes, goannas, emus… This is roo country. That reminds me, I should slow down now." And she did. "I have to watch out for them because they've got no road sense. They just bound right out on to the road."

I saw a lot of birds fly up from a lump on the roadside. "Oh, look!" I said, pointing. "Is that a dead one?"

"Yeah. He's just roadkill now, poor old thing. And that was a wedge-tailed eagle, eating him," she said, pointing to a huge bird that was flapping away. An eagle! It gave me a kind of shiver of excitement to see a real eagle.

I kept looking for live roos but I didn't see one. I was glad. I didn't want one to jump out in front of us and get hit. I saw more dead ones, though, and there were waves of stink in the air.

On and on we drove. At times I thought I might be getting bored, but there was always something new to see. The trees were sort of wonderful. I'd never seen anything like them at home. Gran said, "Pretty well everything here is different from everything anywhere else. It's because Australia was cut off from the rest of the world, millions of years ago, and different kinds of plants and animals evolved. That's what makes this such an exciting, wonderful place. Aren't you glad I brought you?"

Well, I was. At least, I had been, till now. Now we were driving alone through the bush in this clapped-out rusty tin can, which I kind of thought might break down, and Gran had changed. I began to feel just a little bit uneasy. It was pretty obvious we weren't going back to the hotel that night. Maybe not at all.

After about five hours, when I was stiff and starving, we stopped in a little town. It was so different from Perth! Perth is like any big city (only a lot nicer, certainly than London). This was like something out of an old Western movie, except for all the utes parked along the street instead of horses. The buildings had those funny wooden fronts, and the men walking around looked kind of like cowboys, in a way. Gran parked outside a bar and we went in. I was sure someone would say I was too young, but nobody took any notice. There was hardly anyone in this bar place, and it was dark and dreary. As soon as I walked into it, I wanted to leave, but I needed a pee like mad and by the time I got back Gran'd ordered hamburgers and some Cokes. I counted the cans. Five. I looked around to see if anyone else had joined us.

"Who are all the Cokes for, Gran?"

"One for you, four for me. Or, if you're really thirsty, two for you and then I'll have to order another for me."

I'd never seen anyone drink like she did. She just poured it down as if she didn't have to swallow. At the end of each can she'd smack her lips and pick up the next.

"What I couldn't do to a beer!" she said. "But don't you worry, sweet-pants. I'm just rehydrating myself. I wouldn't drink and drive." I didn't say anything. I knew my dad sometimes had, even though he'd never been stopped. Mum used to totally panic… Of course, that was when we *had* an old banger. Needless to say, he took it with him when he left us.

We set off again. I asked where we were going. You'll think it's about time I thought to ask that, but up till then I'd just been kind of going with the flow. I'd got out of the habit of asking questions.

She shouted above the motor, "Can't you guess? We're going to my station."

I gawped at her. I was thinking railway or tube stations, like, Peckham Rye (ours), or Hammersmith (Nan's) or Waterloo. "You've got a *station?*"

"Course I have! I told you about it."

She hadn't. She had not. She'd never mentioned a station. I'd have remembered.

I'd have asked her to tell me more, but the motor was roaring and I felt too exhausted. The country was more like desert now. There weren't so many trees, just these low bushes and big tufts of tall grey grass. There wasn't much to

52

look at, and it was getting hotter and hotter. And dustier. I kept washing the dust out of my throat with one of the big water bottles. At last I fell asleep.

Gran woke me up. It was dark. We must've been driving all day.

"Right, Stacey-bell, out you get and help me make a fire."

I slid out of the cabin and almost fell over a pair of wellies. "Put those on," said Gran. "And take this torch. There's lots of wood around. But be sure you kick it before you pick it up."

"Why?"

"Why d'you think?"

I had no idea why anyone would kick wood. But as I was taking my sandals off to put on the rubber boots, a terrible idea came into my head.

"Gran! Are there snakes around here?"

"There might be. But just remember, the snake that bites you is the one you don't see, so keep a lookout."

Oh my God. I nearly fainted. I already said how I hate snakes. I've always had a thing about them. I don't know why because, like I said before, I'd never seen one. They just give me the creeps.

I shot back into the cabin of the ute and sat there shivering with my legs tucked up, imagining loads of snakes coming slithering right up the step and on to the ute floor. Gran came round to my side. "Get out, Stacey," she said. I think that was the first time she'd called me by my name and not some nickname. And it was the first time I'd heard her use an ordering tone to me. When I still didn't move, she said, "Don't be such a pom."

"What's a pom?" I asked. My teeth were chattering. Honest to God, they were.

"An English person is a pom. Poms have a bad name with us Aussies for being whingers. I'm not having a whingeing pom for a granddaughter. Now get these boots on your feet and get me some wood or there'll be no food."

"I don't want any. I want to go back to sleep."

"We'll make up the beds when we've eaten."

"What beds? I'm not sleeping anywhere near the ground!"

"You're sleeping in the back of the ute. Nothing can get at you there. Come on, now, hurry up, I'm starving." When I still didn't move, she said, "We must make a fire to keep the dingoes away."

I knew dingoes were wild dogs. Dingoes are fierce. I've read about it. They eat babies.

I thought of those movies about African safaris or American cowboys where the campfire keeps wolves and other dangerous animals from coming near. I was so scared, thinking of wild dogs creeping up on us, I almost forgot about snakes. But Gran was just standing there, sort of tapping her foot. I couldn't just sit there scrunched up all night. I *was* a bit hungry, come to think of it. And except for the torch, it was pitch dark. A fire would be good. I slowly unscrunched and stuck my feet out. Gran very briskly pushed the wellies on, then pulled me out and put the torch into my hand.

"Go," she said, turning away.

I shone the torch around and right away I saw some dead wood lying quite close by. I kicked it hard, twice. Nothing popped out. It was a real effort to make myself bend down and snatch up a branch with my finger and thumb. Then I had to walk over to where Gran was digging a sort of pit with a big flat shovel. I shone the torch in front of my boots all the way.

"Here's a piece," I said, dangling it.

She stopped and squinted at it as if it was so small she couldn't see it. "Oh, that's amazing," she said. "Do you think you could possibly find me another one just like it? Then we can rub them together and make sparks."

I dropped the piece and shone my way back to the pile I'd taken it from. I kicked it again. Bit by bit I carried or dragged all the wood from it to where Gran was. She'd pulled up some of the dry grass tufts and before long she'd got a fire going. (Using matches of course. I should've known she was having me on.)

The wood was dry and it really burnt a treat. It was weird how much better I felt as soon as it blazed up. She kept me at it till we had a good woodpile – I had to go further than just right next to the ute to get enough. I kept kicking the wood but there were no snakes and after a bit I got so I wasn't scared to death. I still felt pretty brave though, going off into the dark like that by myself. Once I went about three whole metres from the fire.

By the time Gran was satisfied we had enough wood, there were some hot embers. She scooped them up with the shovel and put them in the pit she'd dug. Then she said, "Now be a love and bring me the Esky."

I wasn't really speaking to her at this point, and I felt silly, asking "What's this" and "What's that" all the time, so I went to the back of the ute. I'd no idea what an Esky was, but I soon guessed, because what do you put food in if it's going to be shone on by the sun all day? One of those cold-box things, right? And sure enough there was one. It was dead heavy. I couldn't get it over the side of the ute so then I noticed there was a kind of catch on the ends of the ute-back. When I slid them, the back fell down with a crash. After that I could drag the Esky off and lug it back to the fire.

Gran opened it and inside were six packages wrapped in foil, along with some milk and tins of Coke. She laid the packets on top of the red embers, then she shovelled more embers on top. The whole thing glowed like an electric stove-plate. She covered the red place with earth and then she got out a thermos and we had some coffee. It was still warm, and sweet. I never drink coffee at home but I drank a big tin mugful.

"That's your pannikin," she said. "I'm giving you that. You can even put it on the fire if you want to heat it up." But I just drank it as it was. The pannikin was pretty, sort of mottled red, and I didn't want the bottom to get burnt, if it was my present. I reckoned I'd earned it, being brave about the snakes and that, and collecting lots of wood.

Then Gran said, "What's that blood on your arm?" Later I wished I'd said, "Oh, nothing, it's just where a dingo bit me," but I just muttered it was a scratch from a sharp bit of wood. She looked at the cut and said, "Well, a whingeing pom would've whinged about that, so good on you." She squeezed it and said, "Good, there's no splinters left in there." Then she got out a jar and started smearing something on the cut.

"What are you putting on it?"

"Honey."

"*Honey!*"

"Sure. Didn't you know honey's an antibiotic?"

"Why do I need an antibiotic?"

"Because that's mulga wood and if you get it stuck in your flesh, it's poisonous."

My mouth fell open – again. Poisonous *wood*? Was there anything safe in this place?

The food took quite a while to cook in the embers. At last a really good smell started to come out of the ground. By the time Gran dug the food out I was like dying of hunger. She'd got two plastic chairs off the ute, and a little folding table, two plastic plates, and knives and forks. And some butter and salt. Gran dusted the ashes off the foil and opened the packets. Inside were big chicken legs, baked potatoes, and cobs of sweet corn. We didn't bother about the knives and forks in the end, we just ate with our fingers by firelight. It tasted well delicious. I drank Coke and she drank beer. Then she stood up and stretched and said, "Right. Bed."

She made me close the Esky and pack all the stuff away in a box. I thought I'd better burn the chicken bones in case they brought the dingoes. The fire was dying down. Nearly all my wood was gone. I said, "Who's going to keep the fire going?"

She said, "Well it's no use looking at Glendine. She's going to make big Zs."

I said, "But if we don't, the dingoes'll come!"

She said, "You're an easy mark, Stacey. There's no dingoes around here. Now help me with my bed."

I didn't say anything. I helped her lift a rusty old iron bed with fold-back legs and a mattress off the back of the ute, and she set it up. It wasn't far off the ground... There was another mattress left on the floor of the ute for me. Then she untied two bundles.

"Here's your swag," she said. A swag turned out to be a sleeping bag. She had a pillow for me, too. She made up her own bed with another swag. I said, "I need to go to the loo." I know I sounded sulky. I couldn't *believe it* about the dingoes, that she'd do that just to make me get out and help.

She picked up the shovel and the torch. "Go ahead," she said. "Over there, by those trees. Keep downwind, ha ha."

I stared at the shovel, thinking what it meant. I had to dig a hole, and— No. It was too gross. Though how else? We were a million miles from anywhere. It looked to me like even the trees were about a hundred miles away from the little circle of firelight where the ute was. Where Gran was.

"Was it true about the snakes?" I said.

"Lovie, would I lie to you? Of course there are snakes in the outback. Just keep shining the torch and stay where the ground's open. Oh, here's some dunny paper. Be sure to bury it, too. Now go on and do what you have to do."

Grandpa used to say, "Needs must, when the devil drives." So I did it. I managed somehow. But the walk there into the darkness was the worst thing I'd ever done, even worse than when our diving teacher made us dive into the school pool over her arm the first time.

I was beginning to change my mind about Gran being the greatest. That's putting it nicely.

Chapter Four

When I ran back to the ute, she was lying on her swag on her bed fast asleep. She hadn't even undressed. I noticed she'd left her boots on one of the plastic chairs. I rinsed my hands and face with water from the bottle, swilled out my mouth, set the other chair against the back of the ute and climbed up. I didn't know whether to undress or what, but my night things were all in my case, so I just dropped my boots over the side and lay down on my swag just as I was. There was a bit of a breeze which made it not so hot. I wished the back of the ute wasn't down, I'd've felt safer with it up. I struggled with it a bit in the dark but I couldn't lift it. If I'd let myself, I could've easily imagined dingoes sniffing me, or... But I fell asleep straight away.

In the night I woke up. It was light that woke me. It'd been completely dark but now there was a pale light all over everything. I lifted myself on my elbows to look and there was the moon, or half of it, just a bit above the horizon but already lighting up the bush and us and everything. There were spooky tree-shapes all around the clearing where we were. I noticed the silence. Total. No birds or anything. It's never, ever that quiet in London.

I lay back down and looked at the sky. Stars! You couldn't just say there were stars, like it was something ordinary. I'd never seen anything like those stars in my life. Billions – and that's no exaggeration. The more you looked at the bright ones, the more tiny little faint ones you could see in between. There didn't seem to be an inch of sky without any. Right overhead there was a thicker path of them. It stretched from one side to the other, like someone had splashed some milk. Suddenly I realised that must be the Milky Way. I'd heard of it but I'd somehow never thought it was real – I thought it was, like, something in *Star Trek*.

There was something *so scary* about that bigness. I couldn't look at it for long. I had to shut my eyes and pretend it wasn't there because I just felt sick to my stomach from all that emptiness with me tiny and helpless underneath it. I filled my own darkness behind my eyelids with Mum's bedroom and Mum's bed with Mum snoring beside me.

Then some real snores started. Gran's. That was some comfort. After a bit I dozed off, but I had terrible, scary dreams. The Milky Way turned into a big white snake, coming out of the sky to get me.

In the morning, bright sunlight and bacon smells woke me.

Gran was tending the fire. There was a blackened old kettle on one bit of it and a blackened old frying pan on the rest. She'd made up a new woodpile. I looked at my watch. It was five thirty. There were plenty of birds about now. They were going mad in fact.

"Hello, Gran," I said, kind of dopily. It seemed funny we were still here and that I wasn't scared any more.

"Hi there, Stace, how are you going? Sleep well?"

"Sort of."

"Want your coffee in bed? Billy's boiling."

I didn't even think "Who's Billy?" I could see that "Billy" was the kettle, and I remembered some song when I was a little kid about "he sang as he watched and waited till his billy boiled", and how I used to think it was his willy that was boiling. I giggled and hiked myself up, leaning my back against the cabin. I just sat there all peaceful, looking around again. There was nothing scary about the bush by

63

daylight, it looked beautiful. The colours were red, for the ground, and a sort of greyey-green for the grass tufts (I found out later it's called spinifex), and brown for the tree trunks. Not all the mulgas were dead, some had leaves on them. And the sky was a gorgeous dark blue. Would you believe the sun was hot already? Gran handed me up my pannikin full of fresh hot coffee.

"Get a swig of that into you and then jump down for breakfast. It'll be ready in a minute."

I wanted to get down right away. I felt suddenly all hot and uncomfortable and I needed to go. I put the pannikin on the roof of the cabin and started to scramble over the side of the ute. Suddenly Gran said, "Hey! Have those boots been on the ground all night? Wait right there." She came and picked them up and shook them, open end down. Something dropped out of one of them.

"Oh, look! You see? I practically saved your life!" she said, all cheerful.

"Why? What is it?"

Whatever it was was scuttling away. It looked like a black prawn with claws and a tail.

"Scorpion," said Gran. "Good it didn't bite you, that would've been the sign of an early spring all right!"

"Kill it, Gran, stamp on it!" I shrieked.

"No! Why kill it? It's only doing its thing."

I watched it darting to and fro on the flat red earth – looking for somewhere to hide, probably.

"Oh, catch it, Gran! I don't want it running around near us!"

Gran laughed and clapped her pannikin upside down on top of the scorpion. I thought of it getting a coffee-bath and straight off felt sorry for it.

I didn't want to climb down after that, but she made me. I wished there was a pathway up above the ground so I wouldn't have to touch anything dangerous. I went off to the trees again. It seemed just as gross as it had the night before – worse cos it was daylight. I thought I'd never get used to going in the open.

The bacon and eggs were good. Gran must've done a load of shopping.

She said, "Today we'll be at the station. You're just going to love it, I bet."

She got me to roll the swags up tight and tie them, and help load everything. Just as she was climbing into the cabin, I thought of something.

"What about your pannikin?"

"Oh! Thanks for reminding me." She started to climb out. "You better sit tight, Stace, or the scorpion might get you!"

"Can we bring him?" I heard myself asking.

"Oh, so it's a *him* now, is it?" She gave me a funny look. "You must be starving for a pet! Have you never had one?"

I shook my head.

"Right, you can bring it along if you can put it in this." She gave me a glass jar. "Let's see how you manage. Need I say, don't touch it?"

Now I had to catch it, I got scared again. I didn't know why I'd said I wanted it. I circled its pannikin prison two or three times. Finally Gran took pity on me.

"Here, I'll show you."

She came over with a piece of cardboard. It looked very thin, like any self-respecting poisonous insect could sting right through it. "Slide it under the mug. Careful… Don't lift the mug too much… That's it, you've got him! Hand underneath, press the mug down tight. Now, bend the card into a little funnel – he can't get up at you – slide him into the jar… right on, you've done it!" And she snatched the jar off the ground and screwed a lid on. I was sweating, literally.

"Can he breathe in there?"

"Every now and then you can unscrew the lid a bit. Good girl, now we've got an extra passenger." She gave me kind of a pleased look.

"What?"

66

"I was just thinking. If you're so keen on creatures that you want a pet scorpion, you are just going to love the station. It's stiff with 'em."

"Scorpions?"

"Among other things."

As we drove I held my scorpion on my knee. I know it sounds crazy, but when I saw him scuttling about inside, I thought it was nice to have a little live thing of my own, even if it would bite me if I touched it. Sting, I mean.

The driving was even longer and rougher that day. We saw some emus. That was fantastic. There was like a family of them, two big ones and three little ones. They kind of tiptoed across the road, a long way in front of us. I let out a shriek and Gran stopped the ute and we watched them till they disappeared. I felt all breathless. They were so huge, for birds!

"I wish I could see them close to."

"You will," Gran said. "I've got two tame ones at home. They lay the most beautiful eggs in the world. A gorgeous greeny-blue colour. The Aborigines carve them like cameos. I've got one at home, I'll show you."

"What's a cameo?"

"A cameo? It's a kind of a – it's sort of jewellery. A two-coloured stone carved into a picture."

Around noon we drove into a little town called Laverton. It was nice, with lots of trees and greenery, and shops and stuff. It was full of black people. Their hair was long and curly. Soft curls, not frizzy. Some of them were very black and some weren't. Probably because their parents had married white people (Loretta's dad was white, but she's still got frizzy hair).

I saw a little girl walking along with her mother. She was dark skinned but she had blonde hair, really yellow. I asked, "Is that little girl an Abo too, Gran?"

"Don't stare," she said, quite sharply. "And don't ever call them Abos. That's really bad manners. They're Aborigines, or Wonngais, to give them the name they call themselves around here. And yes, she is. It's quite usual for the desert kids to have blond hair when they're young." That seemed really interesting. You'd never get a black person at home with blond hair unless they dyed it. But these people hadn't come from Africa or the West Indies.

When Gran'd bought enough supplies we came out of the nice air-conditioned supermarket and she went to collect mail from some post-office box. Woof! What heat! I could feel myself sweating but it seemed to dry right away. I was standing in the shade waiting, batting flies, when a bunch of Aboriginal girls, about my age, went down a sort of alley. And I suddenly saw a sign that said

"Pool" with an arrow pointing behind the shopping centre. I ran to meet Gran.

"Gran, can we swim?"

"Good idea. Let's dig out our bathers."

She'd left the ute parked under a tree. Of course all our stuff was just lying there in the back under the canvas. Anyone could've pinched from it. I thought either Gran was very trusting or the people of this town were very honest, you'd never dare do that in London.

Anyway, we unpacked our swimsuits – mine was my new purple and green bikini – and went for a swim in this gorgeous pool. It was practically Olympic size, it looked like a great big jewel shining in the sun. It had the lanes marked on the bottom. There were quite a lot of people there and lots of noise. The girls I'd seen were just coming out of the changing room as we went in. They weren't wearing proper swimsuits, just sort of shorts with baggy T-shirts over them.

When they saw me coming out of the changing room, they all stopped and looked at me. Kind of nudging and staring. I dived in quickly, wanting to hide from their eyes.

Gran dived straight in and started swimming lengths. Being long and wiry, she didn't look bad in her cossie, considering her age. And she was a very good swimmer. I was thinking of challenging her to a race, but when I saw her front crawl I thought *she* might be able to beat *me*.

One of the black girls was swimming near me. Too near. I gave her a bit of a smile and she did a duck-dive to the bottom. I kept on in my lane and then I felt something underneath me. I opened my eyes underwater and I saw her. She was swimming under me as if I was a boat and she was a whale or something, only she was swimming on her back. Looking up at me.

I started swimming fast to get away from her. She came up and swam fast too, in the lane next to mine. She was amazing. Her crawl was twice as good as mine. Of course, we hadn't agreed to race so I just slowed down. She got to the other end and turned around and laughed, but when I looked straight at her she duck-dived again.

I waited for her to surface. When she did, I said "Hi" but she didn't answer. She just put her face into the water. But every time she had to come up to breathe, she peeped at me. The other girls were swimming around me like dolphins. I couldn't make them out. Were they teasing, or curious, or what? I admit I felt a bit nervous of them. Like they were ganging up on me.

When Gran had had enough, she got out of the pool and called me.

"Come on, we're going."

I got out. "Gran, you see that girl? I was trying to talk to her but she wouldn't."

70

"Too shy I expect."

"Shy?" They hadn't acted shy. "Why?"

"That's just the way they are. Let's get dressed and go."

The girl had climbed out on the other side. She and some of the others were still peeping at me. Every time I looked back at them, they kind of hid their faces. But this one girl, and another one, followed us into the women's changing room. There were no cubicles. I turned my back politely like you do, but they kept going round in front of me and peeping and giggling. It got on my nerves.

"What are you looking at me for?" I finally asked.

One of them nudged the other, the one who'd started racing me. "Where you got that?" she asked, and pointed to my bellybutton ring.

So that's what she'd been looking at, under the water. These girls were just fascinated by it, I could see.

I said, "I got it done at home."

She stared a bit more and then she said, "That your *gubalee*?" She gave a funny little upward jerk of her head towards Gran, like, pointing with her chin.

"What's she saying, Gran, what's a *gubalee*?"

Gran was just pulling on her combat pants and didn't turn round.

"Tell her, yes, I'm your *gubalee*," she said. "It means grandmother."

I said, "She's my gran. I'm visiting her."

"You talk funny way like video," said the other girl.

And the first one said, "Someone musta give you honey ant when you too little." They giggled again.

"They got no honey ants in England," said Gran.

"You from *England?*" the girl almost shouted. "Prince Harry go to your school?"

I thought of him at our school in Peckham, and laughed. "Of course not."

"You know the Queen?" They seemed to have forgotten about being shy. The first one had teeth to die for and lovely curls, quite fair, which looked nice against her dark skin, but still she looked strange to me. I wondered if she thought I looked strange. I sort of wished I had more piercings, to impress them. I said, "What's your name then?"

She giggled and said, "Merinda."

Gran turned round. "Merinda! I didn't know you, you've grown so much! How's your mum? OK?" She nodded. "How's your dad?"

"Good."

"Come into town for stores?"

She tilted her head. Then she looked at me. "You go to Yamarna?"

"Are we, Gran?" I asked.

"Yes we are, and right this minute." She was all ready, hair and everything, and I was still standing there dripping.

Merinda turned to her friend and they began moving their hands, a bit like deaf people. Suddenly they stopped, and I saw Gran was doing it too. They got very embarrassed and went running out, back to the pool. I heard them jump in with two big splashes.

"That showed them," said Gran.

"Do you know their sign language?"

"More or less. They usually use it together with talking, so it's easy to learn. Sometimes they do it when they don't want white fellas to understand. But I told them it was bad manners, saying things about you right in front of you."

"What'd they say?"

"That you were like some movie star."

I pricked up my ears. "Oh? Which one?"

"One with a big wide mouth that won some prize. That's what they signed."

I didn't say anything. As we got back in the ute I thought, *Not Julia Roberts! They couldn't think I look like her!* But it made me feel friendly towards them, that maybe they did.

We had to pick up a big drum of fuel, and some sandwiches and Cokes. Then there were more hours of driving, from

Laverton to the station. It was the hottest time of the day, and there was no shade. The road was just a long, wide, straight road made of red dirt. There was enough room on it for four cars to drive side by side, but we didn't pass anything. Not one single thing. Just us on this unmade motorway. It was crazy.

"Why did they build such a wide road if there's no traffic?" I asked.

"It's for the mining companies."

"What sort of mines?"

"Gold, of course," Gran said.

I sat up. "Gold! Are there gold mines around here?"

"This whole area is a gold mine waiting to happen," she said.

I was half-asleep when I felt a sudden big thump right beside me as if the door was going to burst open inwards, and the ute swerved. As I opened my eyes I saw, just for half a second, a kangaroo's face in my window! Then it was gone. I knew we'd hit it, or rather it had hit us. Gran was looking in the mirror.

"Did we kill him?"

"Looks like it. It's laying there."

"Shouldn't we go back?"

After a second she said, "Yes, we'll have to. I'll do a U-ie."

She did a U-turn, and drove back. We passed the place, stopped and got out. The kangaroo was lying by the side of the road. It was a big grey one, with a paler front. It was alive. And it was a she, I knew because she had a baby in her pouch. I could see its little legs sticking out and I couldn't tell if it was dead or not.

"Turn your back, Stacey," said Gran.

But I couldn't. I kept staring at the kangaroo, who was trying to lift her head and scrabbling with her front paws, like she was begging or praying. Gran took hold of my arm and almost dragged me back to the ute cabin. "Get in," she said. I did and she shut the door. But I looked in the mirror. Gran took something off the back of the ute. It was a piece of metal, some kind of tool. Then she went back to where the mother kanga lay. I honestly didn't know until she lifted the rod-thing what she was going to do.

I got such a shock when she brought it down on the poor thing's head that I just hid my eyes. I sat there all hunched up, trying not to hear anything. I thought, *This is the worst. This place is horrible. Gran's horrible.* But I knew she wasn't, that she had to kill it to put it out of its pain. But what about the baby? She wasn't going to beat that to death too, was she?

After a bit, Gran got into the driving seat. I heard her, but I wasn't looking. I was still all scrunched up with my eyes screwed shut. She didn't say anything. She just sat there, and after a couple of minutes I heard the scratch of a match. I looked up quickly. Yes, she was lighting a cigarette! I'd never seen her smoke before, and she'd often told Mum off for smoking in front of me. Her hands were shaking.

She glanced at me and muttered something about hating to do it like that, but I wasn't listening. I was sort of numb. She took a couple of drags and then threw the fag out of the window. I came out of my numbness.

"Gran! You're not going to leave it there!"

She didn't ask what. She said, "What do you think."

"Can we keep it?"

"Stacey, no. You can't keep the joey. They're a damn nuisance. You'd have to raise it on the bottle. It'd probably die anyway."

"But we killed its mum! It'll starve if we don't take it!" I was thinking of my toy, when I was little, my Kanga and Roo toy. I'd loved it so much. I'd taken it to bed with me for years. I still had it as a matter of fact, somewhere. I thought, *If Gran drives away and leaves that baby for the eagles and crows I'm never going to speak to her again.*

But what Gran said was, "We're not going to leave it to starve. I don't like killing them like this, but I've got to."

I felt devastated. After a moment I said, in a breathless sort of voice, "Please don't kill it. Please let me keep it."

Gran was staring at me. Finally she said, "Will you look after it? Cos I haven't time or patience." That made me think. I didn't know how to look after a baby kangaroo. I said, "Yes I will if you tell me how." She said, "OK, here's how it starts. It needs to be warm and safe, so you've got to be its mother. When I bring it to you, here's what you do. You tuck your top into your pants and you kneel down and pull the front of your top away from your body. When the joey sees that, he'll jump right in there."

"Into my *top*!" I screamed. "You mean I've got to keep it next to my *skin*?"

"Yes," she said, still looking at me.

"But it'll scratch and bite!"

"No it won't."

"It'll – it'll pee on me, or crap."

"It won't do that either. I'll show you how to house-train it, I mean skin-train it. Only, Stacey, if it's a male, you can't keep him. They get stroppy and dangerous quite early. You can keep it if it's a female, that's if you want to. I'm going now to look."

We both got out again. I didn't want to, but I felt feeble, sitting there while Gran did everything. If the baby was going to be mine I ought to be there. But it was *well* horrible seeing that poor dead kanga with her head all bloody.

The baby had huddled down into the pouch, poor little thing. Gran reached down and gathered it up by the neck and the feet, and pulled it out quite gently. She put her hand under its back as if she was holding a baby. She cradled it and it kind of settled down, with its pointed nose stuck in her armpit. It was about the size of a big skinny cat, but with these two long, spindly back legs and a long strong-looking tail. I held my breath. What would we do if it was a boy? I wouldn't let Gran kill it, or the crows have it – I wouldn't! Gran took a quick look and smiled.

"It's a doe, Stace. Do you want her or don't you?"

A baby kangaroo to look after! A pet of my very own… I never let myself think that in two weeks I'd have to leave it. I just looked at it, all furry and soft and with its little eyes looking at me, and its long dangly legs, and its dead mum lying there and I was, like, just one big YES.

There was no room in my top for anything but me, but Gran lent me one of her shirts. I buttoned it and tucked it into my jeans. Gran put the baby on the ground and I crouched down and pulled the neck of my shirt forward with two fingers. The joey got on her back legs and jumped in head first. Next thing, she was down around my stomach somewhere. It felt so funny! All warm and furry, but at the same time wriggly and scratchy. I could feel her sort of settling down, and then I felt her start to lick my tummy. It tickled like mad and I burst out laughing.

"She'll lick the salt off your skin," said Gran. "Come on, we'd better get going."

For the last hour of the drive I just kept my hands on the baby through the shirt. She was an orphan. Sort of like me in a way. I felt her licking and nuzzling me. I just fell in love with her. She was all mine – the sweetest little animal in the whole world.

"She's hungry, Gran, she's nuzzling me."

"She's probably not hungry yet. She'll have had a feed recently. The teats are inside the pouches, of course." She gave a snort. "I hope she doesn't start sucking that silly ring-thing on your bellybutton, she won't get much joy out of that! I'll give you a bottle of milk when we get home." After a bit she said, "I've got some lactose-free milk somewhere from when some tourists came through with a baby roo they'd found, only it died on them."

The little joey started trembling as if she'd heard. I stroked her soothingly. "Will she die, Gran?"

"She's well-furred already, almost ready to come out of the pouch anyway. She should be OK."

After another long while she said, "There's another pet you might like, just ahead."

I looked. It was a great big snake! It was squirming across the road very fast. I felt my heart jump, but I didn't let myself feel scared because I knew it couldn't get at us. But still I said, "Run it over, Gran!" She could have, easily, but instead she slowed down till it'd got across.

"No point killing for nothing," she said, like she had with the scorpion.

My scorpion! Where was it? I looked round in a panic, and then saw the jar on the floor. I said, "Gran, I don't really want the scorpion now. Can we let it go?"

She braked the ute. "Give it to me then," she said, and got out and let it free by the side of the road. "I hope you don't fall in love with Humpy White and give up on the joey," she said as she got back in.

"Who?"

"He's my tame baby wild camel."

"How can he be tame *and* wild?"

"He's wild and I've tamed him!"

"You said there were no regular animals in Australia."

"These are Afghan camels, they were brought in to help carry supplies for the early settlers. When gold was discovered, they lugged gear for the gold mines. Then their owners bought trucks and left the camels to go wild. You know that girl you met at the pool, Merinda? Her great-grandfather was an Afghan cameleer."

"Do you know her?"

"I know Alexis and Wombley, her mother and father, and her grandfather. He's called Brando, after Marlon Brando. Lots of them are named after famous white people."

"Who's Marlon Brando?"

She looked at me as if she didn't believe she'd heard right. Then she shook her head.

"You make me feel so old," she said. Don't know what she meant by that.

It was mid-afternoon when we finally turned off the road and drove along a dirt track for about a mile. On each side of us was just more desert, not empty desert but red sand dotted with low bushes and a few mulga trees, mostly dead. Then I saw the station.

I don't know what I was expecting. Maybe I still thought some grand building like Waterloo or St Pancras would suddenly pop out of the horizon. Anyway, when I saw it it seemed just like part of the scenery. It was a bunch of small buildings, sort of huddled in the middle of nowhere. There was a bungalow, some cattle pens, a strange thing like a square arch made of metal pipes, and a few little shacks and sheds gathered around a big yard. It looked as if someone'd built a house, then found they needed some other buildings and just knocked them together and stuck them around any old how. There was a lot of junk, too, rusty old stuff strewn around in heaps.

The only thing that stood up tall, apart from the pipe-arch and a few trees, was a windmill. It looked like a small pylon and it had lots of little sails, not just four like the Dutch ones. They were whizzing around in the hot wind. There was another truck parked outside the bungalow. It looked a bit newer than ours.

There were hens running around, scratching and pecking. And – wow, could I trust my eyes? – two great big birds, pecking along with them, like giants among dwarves. Emus!

Gran leant out of the window. "Here, Dora! Here, Nora! Come say hello to Stacey!"

And would you believe it, they came! These two huge balls of feathers with their long scrawny necks and the *funniest* little heads that would make you laugh just to look at them, came running to the ute like stilt walkers on their long legs. Gran grabbed the remains of a stale sandwich, tore it in half and fed them as they stuck their heads right into the window. It was hard to believe I was really seeing it. I swear they were *grinning* at her. No, not grinning. Smiling. Like girls. They had girlie faces with great long eyelashes.

Gran climbed out. I could see she was stiff and tired. She stroked the emus' necks and then said to me, "Come on, Stace, this is it. We're home!"

She didn't wait for me. She just pulled the Esky out of the back, went stumbling up the steps to a sort of porch and disappeared through a door that banged behind her. I got out more slowly because I was still holding Roo. That's what I'd decided to call her. I know Roo in the stories was a boy, but so what.

If I'd thought it'd been hot so far, on the journey, I found out now what real hot is. I felt as if I'd been hit on the head, like that poor kanga, except it was the sun falling on me. I just stood there supporting Roo. I thought, *I should have a hat on. I should get indoors.* But I was, like, stunned. I couldn't move at all at first. It was only when an emu came too close that I stirred myself to walk very slowly and carefully after Gran. The emus followed me and I should've been a bit scared of them, they were so big, but with the sun hitting me I hadn't the energy to be scared.

I climbed up the sagging wooden steps very slowly and across this open porch place, with a very old swing seat on it, and went in through a screened door.

Right inside the door was the living room, with Gran lying on a red sofa with her feet up and her eyes closed. She'd kicked her cowboy boots off. "I'm knackered, Stace," she said. "All of a sudden it's hit me. Your room's through there. I need a rest."

"What about Roo's milk?"

83

"Roo? Oh, Roo. OK. You'll find a baby's bottle in one of the cupboards in the kitchen. The milk should be in the fridge. It's powdered. You'll need to add warm water. And bring Glendine a beer, eh? There's a little angel."

The kitchen opened off the living room. What a place. Our kitchen at home was bang spanking modern and clean compared to this. I couldn't believe the mess. Surely Gran hadn't just left it like this, weeks ago? The sink was full of pots and dirty dishes and every flat surface was covered with stuff. I found a jar of dried milk marked "Digestalac" in the back of the fridge, and mixed some with warm water from the tap. It felt as if it was warm not because it'd been heated, but just because in this weather it couldn't possibly be cold. There wasn't a single clean bowl or anything I could mix it in, so I washed out a little saucepan. The stuff in the bottom of it wasn't dried. Somebody must be living here that Gran hadn't told me about.

I rummaged around in the cupboards for the bottle. They were full of every kind of junk, not just kitchen junk either, there were tools and medicines, tins and boxes of rusty stuff, nails and bits and pieces, and I even found a blowtorch under the sink, but no bottle. I thought I'd take Gran her beer (which I found in the fridge), and ask her again. But when I did, she was zonked out. So I drank it myself. I must say it tasted good, but maybe anything cold and liquid would have.

I was just going back into the kitchen when I heard footsteps. I turned round, and there, just coming in a door at the back, was a stranger. Well, of course he was a stranger. I felt a bit scared. I mean, who could he be, way out here?

He was old, about sixty, with thin grey hair and just a very ordinary old-man's face, all red-brown from the sun. But he had an amazing body. His shoulders and arms were massive, full of muscle, even if it was beginning to be a bit scrawny. The rest of him wasn't so much, he had a belly, and he wasn't very tall. He looked like he'd been a boxer. He was dressed like some old farmer or something, I mean an Australian one, with shorts, boots on his bare legs and a floppy hat. He stopped dead, as if I was the last thing on earth he expected to see.

"Bloody hell, you scared the life out of me! Who are you?" he asked in a very surprised voice.

"I'm Stacey."

"Stacey! What, her grandkid that she's staying with in London?" He seemed in a daze.

"Was. She's here now."

"HERE! You're having me on!"

He threw down some dirty old junk he'd been holding, right on the floor, and went into the living room. I followed him. He was standing there staring down at Gran lying fast asleep on the red plush sofa.

"I don't believe this," he muttered, scratching his bristly chin. "The woman's nuts, that's what. She's crazy." He turned and shooed me on to the porch-place ahead of him. He stood there staring at me. The first thing he noticed was Roo making a wriggly spiky bulge in my shirt.

"What've you got in there, apart from you?"

I felt myself going red. "It's a joey," I said.

He let his mouth fall open. He looked really comic. "That's all I need! A mad woman who never tells a bloke anything, and a kid with a bloody roo jumping about in her clothes!" And he went stamping down the steps. I saw him striding across the yard to the ute, and begin to unload it in a cross kind of way, just flinging things down on the ground.

I thought perhaps I ought to go and help him, but I wanted to feed Roo first. I looked in some more cupboards and finally found the feeding bottle right at the back. It had a rubber teat with something like a bicycle-tyre valve sticking out of it. That must be special for joeys. I poured the warm milk into the bottle and managed to get the teat back on. By this time Roo was scrambling about. She did get hold of my belly-ring in her mouth and gave it a good tug. That hurt and made me hurry, but I thought, *It's like she's ringing the bell for dinner.*

I stuck the bottle down my front and right away she grabbed it in her mouth and started sucking. I found an old chair and sat down in it. I thought, *This is a bit like having a baby to nurse.* I held Roo with my arm under her and I could feel her front feet, which had quite sharp claws on them, kind of holding on to my bra-top.

After a bit the man came back in. He had a load of our sunflower cases and he looked really bad-tempered. But when he saw me with this baby's bottle stuck down the front of my shirt, he couldn't help giving a bit of a laugh.

"Which of these bits of technicolour is yours?"

I pointed.

"I'm taking it into the spare room," he said, and went. He came right back though. "I suppose she's been driving all day and all night like a lunatic?"

"We stopped off in Laverton."

"Did she get some supplies and fuel and collect the mail?" I nodded. "Oh well, that's a relief, so she hasn't lost her mind completely." And he disappeared again.

After I heard him go outside, I went looking for the room I was to sleep in. I liked it right away, which was surprising, because it was dead plain. There was a double bed with nothing on the mattress except a bare pillow, a rug on the wooden floor, a table and chair, a chest of drawers, a cupboard, and a couple of lamps. There were no curtains, just the flyscreens. I looked out. Desert – no, bush – baking in the sun… I started unpacking, but Roo really got in the way so I put her on the floor. She sat up on her haunches and we looked at each other.

"Hi Roo," I said. "Welcome to your new home. Meet your new mum." And I stroked her little bony head and her big ears. Her dark grey fur was as soft as a kitten's. Then I stroked down her back and along her tail, which was thick near her body and thin at the end. I was stroking it when she suddenly crapped on the rug. Little pellets, like a rabbit. Well, that was good, anyway, easy to clean up.

"Bad girl," I said.

She looked at me all bright-eyed as if she'd been dead clever.

When I opened the cupboard to start putting things away I found it was stuffed full already. Junk seemed to be what this place was about. There were piles of sheets and towels and old clothes, and the bottom was full of boots and boxes of stuff – I couldn't tell what it all was. There was no room for anything of mine, anyway. But I found some old wire clothes-hangers and by leaving the door of the cupboard a bit open I could hang some of my clothes. Next, I tried the chest of drawers. By shifting some of the stuff in them I emptied one drawer, and that was mine. I had to leave a lot of my new clothes in my suitcase.

I had to be careful because Roo kept hopping up behind me, nearly making me fall over her. It was so incredibly sweet how she hopped. She just followed me around. She knew she was mine. I kept stopping to pet her. I was crazy about her. My very own kangaroo! I couldn't believe how lucky I was.

More than anything else, though, I needed a shower right now.

I went exploring. The house was quite small. It seemed to be made of some kind of ridged metal sheets for the walls. There were four real rooms, the living room, my room, another bedroom I just peeped into, and the kitchen. There was no bathroom. No bathroom?!

Just then I heard Gran calling me sleepily from the sofa.

"Stacey! Where are you?"

I went in there. "I'm here, Gran."

"Are you OK? I'm sorry I fell asleep. Did you find the milk all right?"

"Yes."

"Did she drink it?"

"Yes. Look how she follows me around!"

Gran sat up a bit and looked behind me at Roo, who was sitting up with her front feet sticking out from her little furry chest.

"All right, Stacey, here are the rules. She can stay in the house till dark and then you have to hang her up on the veranda."

"Hang her up – what d'you mean?"

"I'll give you a pillowcase for her. You must hang it on the door knob, just a little bit open. We'll pad it with old clothes to be comfy for her. Show her the opening at the top, and in she'll go."

"But I want her in bed with me!"

"Not on your life. She has to sleep on the veranda."

"Gran, I'm afraid she crapped in my room."

"Well, there you go! Did you touch her tail or between her back legs?"

"Her tail."

"That's what did it. Look, I'll show you. Now you've got to be a real mum to her or you can't keep her. One crap I forgive, but I can't have her doing her business around the house, Dave'll have my guts for garters."

Dave. I'd forgotten the strange man.

"Gran, a man was here."

"Yeah, that's Dave. Now, this is what mother kangaroos do. They lick their babies between the legs—"

"GRAN!"

"No, *you* don't have to do that. Just touch her – you can use dunny paper – and that stimulates her to go. Of course you take her outside, and you have to do it after she's had her bottle, regularly."

"UGH! I don't want to touch her there, that's gross!"

90

"Right, I'll just take her out and kill her then. What happened to my beer?"

"I drank it."

"Did you! We'll make an Aussie out of you yet."

"Gran, where's the bathroom?"

"We haven't one. Not a proper one. There's the dunny out there." She pointed through the window to a little hut-thing. "For showers, you go into the wash house. Here, I'll show you."

She took me out the back door and across a sort of raised path made of wooden slats, just above the rough ground, with a roof over it. Then we were in another bit of building. It was one room, with a concrete floor. It had a washing machine in it and, over in a corner, a kind of shower arrangement that was just a pipe, a drain underneath, and a plastic curtain on a rail.

"D'you want a shower now? I'll fill the tank for you. You'll have to give me a hand."

She took a couple of enormous plastic bottles and gave me one. We went over to the windmill. There was an old iron bath there full of water, which was quite warm, almost hot, from the sun. We had to dip the bottles in – force them under, really – and fill them, then take them back to the wash house. Then came the incredible part. There was a ladder leaning against the side of the building. Gran tied a rope to the handle of one bottle, and carried the end of the rope up the ladder. Then she stood on the roof, hauled the bottle up, and emptied it into a thing like a metal barrel, over where the shower was. After that she dropped the rope down and I had to tie it to the handle of the second bottle and she hauled that up.

She climbed down again. She was sweating of course. I said, "Gran, please don't tell me you have to do that every time anyone wants a shower."

"Of course," she said. "Dave does it usually, but when he's not here, I do it."

"Who *is* Dave?"

"Dave's – well, he kind of works for me. This is a cattle station, and it's useful sometimes to have help with the heavy work."

"A *cattle* station! You mean, a ranch?"

"We call it a station. We have two hundred head of cows."

"Where are they?"

"Oh, out and about."

"You mean, they're wandering about in the desert?"

"Yeah."

"So how do you – you know, look after them?"

"They do that. All we have to do, most of the time, is make sure they've got enough to drink."

"How?"

"Windmills. We have windmills every 8 k or so that pump up water out of the ground into tanks. The cows know where to go when they need a drink. The problem is that sometimes the windmills break down or seize up. Specially ours, because they're so old. Dave or I have to do the rounds of all our mills regularly so as to make sure they're working, and if they're not, fix 'em. I expect that's where he is now. And talking of drinks, do you fancy another beer?"

I had my shower. I longed for a cold one but the water was muggy-hot. Within five minutes I was pouring sweat again, at least it felt like it but the air was so dry it just evaporated. The heat was really — you couldn't describe it. You could hardly stand it. I didn't understand how people lived out here, never mind worked.

The other bad thing was the flies. They were everywhere. I seemed to spend half my energy brushing them away. I thought the flies alone could drive you crazy in this place.

When I went to look for her, Gran was in the kitchen cleaning up. She didn't complain about the mess, she just set about washing dishes and cleaning the floor, which was covered with some kind of hard stuff, worn away in places. I knew I should help her but I couldn't. I was just, like, zonked out.

"Is it always this hot here, Gran?"

"Is that a whinge by any chance?"

"Maybe it is. I can't help it."

"It's only like this in the summer. You know everything's upside down here, even the seasons."

"I don't know if I'm going to be able to stand this heat."

Gran leant on the mop, wiped her face, and gave me a comic look. "That's bad. So what do you suggest?"

"I don't know."

"Take Roo and go out to the shade house for a bit."

She showed me the shade house. It was a five-sided hut-thing made of poles covered with sacking, and it had a hosepipe at the top that ran water down it. The sacking got soaked and that was supposed to cool the inside. It only worked if there was a bit of a breeze. The rest of the time, it was like a sauna. But at least you were out of the glare of the sun. I lay down on a metal camp bed like Gran'd slept on, and tried to forget I was being slowly roasted to death. Roo being in my shirt again didn't exactly help. The flies were using me as some kind of skating rink.

I slept for a bit and when I woke up I was in a puddle of sweat. I couldn't move. I just lay there. The only bit of me that was working was my brain. Almost since I'd left England, I'd been kind of in a trance of newness and enjoying myself, and just being glad to get away. Now, my thoughts were suddenly quite sharp.

How come Gran'd changed so much? She really was like two people. I couldn't reckon this new Glendine, the bush one. How could one person be so different? Had she just been pretending to be the poshed-up one? Had she somehow been in disguise, and was this the real her?

There was another thing. Until only two days ago, she'd seemed to have pots of money. The ten-quid tips, all that swish luggage, the expensive gear, the outings in London, the stuff she'd bought me, the trip she'd paid for. The hotel. The taxis. The meals. And now this! Talk about a contrast! Hauling the water for a shower up on to a roof by hand. Doing all her own housework in the boiling heat. Having a dunny. A dunny! I was going to have to investigate that very soon. I hadn't had to go so far because I was sweating it out. But I dreaded it. An outdoor toilet... Nan said she remembered having one, before the war, when she lived in Shepherd's Bush, but I'd never even heard of anyone who had one nowadays. Even poor people in the UK have proper plumbing. Don't they? But actually I'd never known any really poor people. Even though we never had hardly any money, I knew we weren't really *poor*.

This was my idea of really poor.

Roo started tugging on my bellybutton ring (ding ding!) and that meant I had to get up somehow and go back into the house and feed her. It was so hot I just wanted to die. How was I going to get through *two weeks* of this? I wasn't sure I could get through one *day*. Maybe it'd get cooler when the sun went down. My geography teacher said it gets very cold at night in deserts. Something to do with the sand. Cold? Cold would be like heaven!

Chapter Five

I dragged myself out of the shade house. I'd taken my sandals off. Not that it made much difference. Roo didn't follow me so I had to carry her. It was like hugging a hot-water bottle.

I met Gran on the porch.

"I was just coming to find you," she said. "It's time to feed the chooks. I thought that might be one of your little jobs." Then she saw my feet. "My God, Stace, don't walk about barefoot – not even in the house."

"Why not?"

"There are lots of biters and stingers around."

"But not indoors?"

"Don't count on it! I shot a dugite last summer. It was hiding under the settee."

"What's a dugite?"

"Don't ask," she said, from which I guessed it was a snake. "And those sandals aren't much protection. Where are the boots I gave you?"

"I need the toilet," I said.

"Ah! Wait a minute." And she disappeared into the house. I stood there in the hot shade. I put Roo down and she started licking my leg, all loving, but I wished she wouldn't.

Gran came back with some more boots. I put them on and we walked to the dunny.

"Must make sure there are no redbacks, ha ha!" she said, leading the way.

"What's a redback?"

"Spider." She started to sing a jolly little song about a redback spider on a toilet seat that bit somebody's bottom. "One bite and you've had it. So you have to look out."

She opened the wooden door. The smell – even though it was mainly disinfectant – stopped me in my tracks.

It was dead primitive, just a sort of cupboard on the ground. The door closed with a hook-and-eye thing. It was a real toilet – I mean, it wasn't a plank with a hole in it – but there was no way to flush. Instead there was a bucket of water to throw down the bowl.

Gran looked all around on the floor and walls. She said I must always do that. If I saw any spiders, especially ones with red backs, I had to chase them away or swat them with a fly-swatter that hung there. I said, "What if they come up the hole while I'm on it?" She laughed and said, again, "That'd be the sign of an early spring!" (This was her favourite joke. Even when I got it – she meant, you'd "spring" into the air – I didn't feel like laughing.) By this time I'd stopped wanting to go. All the "go" I wanted was to go home.

Still, I managed somehow, though I was scared all the time. I didn't even let myself sit on the seat properly. Gran waited for me outside.

"Now you use that hose to fill up the bucket for the next person," she said. "Of course you don't need to flush every time. Just when—"

"All right, Gran! I get it!"

"If it's yellow, let it mellow. If it's brown, flush it down," she said, the way you might say some funny little jingle from a TV advert.

I pretended I hadn't heard her. I mean, *disgusting* or what? I wondered what Nan would say if she heard that!

After I'd refilled the bucket and put it back, I found Gran near a sort of wired-in pen at one end of the yard. OK, so chooks were chickens. They'd all seen where she was going, and they'd come running after her from all around. There were sort of boxes at one end of the pen. Gran opened one

99

of the lids, and reached under a hen that was sitting there. The hen fluffed herself up and pecked Gran's wrist, but she took no notice and brought out an egg. She put it in my hand. It was still warm, but at least it wasn't sticky.

"Put it in your pocket. But don't forget it's there!"

She found three more eggs. Then she gave me some grain in a pan and told me to scatter it. They sort of mobbed me and I was a bit scared, but when I flung the stuff about they just pecked the grain, not me.

"This is your job from now on," she said. "Feeding 'em and collecting the eggs. Every afternoon, OK?"

"Won't they peck me if I take their eggs?"

"Yeah maybe, but it doesn't hurt." She opened the lid of another box. "Here, this is Maisie, she's real gentle. You can stroke her."

I put my hand very cautiously into the box and the hen sat still and let me stroke her. Her back felt like bumpy satin.

"Now, you see? You can reach under her and take her egg."

I was scared. But I did it. Her feathers underneath were soft and warm. I felt the egg. It was kind of exciting, like fishing for something in a lucky dip. I just had my hand on it when the hen's head moved like lightning and it pecked my wrist. I snatched my hand away and the egg flew out and broke on the ground.

"Ah! Poor Maisie! Did she break your egg?"

I felt stupid. I said, "Sorry, I'm not used to it."

"You'll catch on."

"Can we please go indoors now?"

As we went towards the house, we passed near the big metal arch. Gran saw me looking at it.

"That's my gantry. For unloading things. I made that with me little welder."

I stared up at this great metal object. It was at least three metres high. "*You* made that?"

"Oh, not recently," she said. "I don't think I could do that now. When I first came here with your grandpa. He was a lazy mongrel. Never did a hand's turn if he could manage not to. I did most of the hard work in those days. Now, with Dave, it's different, I can take it easy."

We climbed on to the veranda. I managed to hurry a little. I felt sure it must feel cooler in the house, but it hardly did. Gran said, "You look a bit crook, Stace. Go and lie down or something. Put a wet towel on you, that'll cool you down. I'll call you when it's tea time."

I don't remember much more about that first day, till the evening. I know I kept longing for the sun to go down so it'd get cooler. But when it did, it didn't. Well, a bit, but not nearly enough.

One good thing, I had managed to sort myself out a bit in my room before I collapsed, stumbling about in a sort of heat daze. I'd put my things away and laid out my hairbrush and stuff. I cleaned up after Roo. Then I made my bed, just two sheets Gran said, one under, one over, and a pillowcase, all from the stuffed cupboard. Gran showed me how to close the shutters on my window. She said I should keep them closed all day to keep the sun out. I said it would keep the breeze out too, but she said, "What breeze?"

Dave came home for tea. Gran made us some kind of fry-up. I couldn't face it. I thought of salad. I hate salad at home, and never dream of eating it for school dinners, but now I thought of fresh crisp lettuce and icy cold cucumber and sweet tomatoes. I looked at all the greasy food on my plate and I just pushed it away. Dave said, "Don't you want this?" When I said no, he ate it. He was wearing a very old ragged vest that clung to his muscles. I have to say it – he ponged. He *obviously* hadn't had a shower since he came in.

They talked about windmills all through the meal. Boring or what? Roo sat beside me and I tried to feed her bits, but she didn't like it any better than I did. After she'd had her evening bottle I took her out and toileted her like Gran'd told me. I used toilet paper for the stroking. It worked! I was sort of amazed. I bet human mothers would be glad if it was that simple with babies.

Gran was watching me from the veranda. "Good girl, Stace," she said. "That's the way."

I came up the steps slowly and lifted Roo up. There was this kind of double swing seat there, with a very tatty, faded cover. Me and Gran kind of slumped down on to it and rocked it slowly with our heels while the sun went down, a big red ball in the clear sky. When I put Roo up beside me she tried to get into my shirt, but I didn't cooperate and after a bit she gave up and just curled up next to me.

"Have you always lived on the station – like, when my dad was little?" I asked. I tried to sound careless, but really I was dead curious and a bit suspicious by now, after my thoughts in the shade house.

"No. I lived in Melbourne for a while," she said. "It's a beautiful city, Melbourne. *Far* nicer than Sydney, and don't let any Sydneysiders tell you different."

"I don't know any."

"Well, if you did, they'd tell you Sydney's better than Melbourne."

"Did you have a house there?"

"Yeah, a posh one."

"Have you still got it?"

"No! Had to sell it."

A clue? "Why?" I asked carelessly, pushing heel-and-toe.

"I reckoned here was better," she said. She glanced at me. "How do you like the station so far?"

I didn't want to say I thought it was the grottiest place I'd ever seen, so I said, "Where are all the creatures you said about?"

"Let's start with the handy ones. Of course you'll think the emus are more exciting than the chooks, but you can get really fond of chooks. Every one of them came out of its egg right here and I know them all by name. Then there are the cattle, of course. Wait till you meet Spotty! She's my favourite, tame as anything – if I don't watch her she'll march straight into the house."

"Where are they?"

"Out bush now. But when they're here for a muster, you get to love 'em. It's really hard to send them to market."

"But I thought you meant wild things."

"Goannas wild enough for you? And perenties, they're another kind of big lizard. They're beautiful, and they get quite tame – I like having them around because they keep the snakes away. Of course," she added thoughtfully, "the snakes keep the *mice* away."

I shuddered. I don't know which I hated the thought of

most, snakes or some dirty big lizard. I wasn't too happy about the mice, either. "What else?"

"Wild camels. I'm crazy for camels! And then there are tons of birds and smaller things, snakes, spiders, beetles, not all dangerous. Sorry we don't have any koalas, you need to go to a wildlife sanctuary for them." I didn't say anything. She put her arm around me. "Trust me, darling, you'll love it when you get used to it! Don't you want an adventure?"

"It's so hot," I mumbled.

She took her arm away. "No whingeing now! I'll give you a fan for your bedroom, but you know, we don't have a proper electrical supply. We have our own generator. It runs on diesel and we have to bring that in from town. So we don't use it more than we have to. We switch it on for a few hours at night for lights, and then switch it off before we go to bed."

I imagined myself getting up in the dark to go to the dunny at night. Even with the big torch I'd seen out there, I might miss the redbacks and the snakes.

I didn't want to think about that. So I said, "Does the fridge run off the generator?"

"No, kerosene. We can't keep switching *that* off, we'd get warm English beer!"

"Does the TV run on kerosene, too?" I asked.

She said, "What TV?"

My heart seemed to flop down into my shoes. *No TV?* All my favourite soaps were Australian, how could she not have a TV? How could anybody? She had to be kidding! But she wasn't, because she went on, "I only wish we did! That's something I really miss. Of course, I had one in Melbourne, in fact I had three, but here we'd need a satellite dish and I just don't think I'd know how to put it together. Dave's good at most things but he hates technology."

I thought, *But you're rich, why don't you get someone to come out and fix it for you?*

"But you said you had a computer."

"It's only good for word processing. Of course I can't get on the Internet or have email here with no phone."

If I'd been shocked about no TV, think how I felt about no phone! "How can you be right out here and not have a phone?" I almost shouted.

"We had one," she said, "a phone box, outside, it worked with solar panels. But it fell down in a tornado months ago and we haven't been able to fix it."

For a moment I was stopped by the word tornado. *Tornadoes too!* But the phone mattered more. "But Gran, it's dangerous! What if something happened, a redback bit you or you were ill or something?" *Or I was,* I thought. I felt panicky again.

"Ah, well, we have the radio. I ought to show you how to work it, in case you ever need to call the RFDS for me."

"What's that?" I asked.

"The Royal Flying Doctor Service. Don't tell me you've never heard of the Flying Doctor!" I imagined one flying through the air like Mary Poppins with his little bag, and that did make me laugh. Gran said, "Nothing funny about the Flying Doctor, we'd all be up the creek without them."

But I'd stopped listening. I'd suddenly thought of something that hadn't even crossed my mind before, but now it seemed desperately important.

"If we've got no phone, how can I phone Nan and tell her where I am in case Mum comes back?"

There was a silence. She was giving me a sort of gentle look, as if she was sorry for me. "D'you really think she's coming back, Stacey?" she asked quietly.

My heart gave a great jump in my chest. In a flash I thought of going home and having to live by myself, only I wouldn't be allowed to, Social Services would come and take me into care.

"Of course she is!" I shouted. "She wouldn't leave me alone!"

"What if she couldn't leave your dad?"

I felt totally confused. I'd never, ever thought she might not come back. But I knew she was still in love with him –

the mongrel. I stared at Gran and she started to blur. She put her arm around me.

"Poor Stacey," she said. "You're homesick. And you're worried. Of course you are! But if you cry you'll set me off. I can't stand thinking about your dad and mum running out on you. I know how it feels, being dumped…" Running out on me! Being dumped! Every word just seemed to jab my heart. "I want to give you a good time to make up for it. A good, *different* time. Something you'll always remember."

She smiled at me. I sort of smiled back through my tears and she said, "Is there anything I can do for you to make you feel better?"

I thought of saying, "Yes, you can take me home, or back to the hotel in Perth," but that'd sound like a whinge, and anyhow I knew she wouldn't. So I said, "Yes. You could put some lippy on."

She goggled at me in surprise. "I never wear make-up on the station! You just sweat it right off again."

"*Please*, Gran."

She didn't say anything for a minute and I thought she was going to be annoyed. But then she relaxed and smiled. "Oh, all right, just for you!"

She disappeared into the house and, after a bit, she came out again. She'd put on some of her purple eye shadow as well as a great splash of red lipstick. The rest of her face was shiny, but she at least looked a bit like she had in London. She fluffed out her blue hair (which I noticed now had grey roots).

"Is that what you wanted?" she asked.

I said, "Yes. It's just, you look so different here, I felt lonely. Do I have to learn about the radio now?"

"Not tonight, it's too late and you're whacked, I can see. The heat is a bit much, but kids get used to it quickly. Have another shower. I'll do you a cold one this time, I'll pump it up for you, then you and Roo can get an early night. I'll get her pillowcase and you can put her to bed."

I don't know how I slept, even after a cool shower, but I was knackered like she said, and she did give me a fan. I opened the shutters because I thought there *must* be a bit of a breeze, and there was, but there was also moonlight like the night before. In the middle of the night it woke me up again. The fan had stopped and the heat lay on me like a blanket. I kicked off the sheet and lay there with nothing on.

I started wondering if Roo was all right. I'd given her a bottle and she'd hopped into the padded pillowcase, earlier. But maybe she was lonely. A pillowcase isn't a bit like a mum. I wondered if she knew, like, sensed, that her mum was dead. Thinking about the kanga made my insides twist up. I started one of those stupid awake-dreams I get caught up in sometimes, like I'm making up a movie. It was because Gran'd hinted Mum might never come back. My fantasy got out of control. My mum died in it... I started crying. I wanted to cuddle Roo. For my sake now.

I got up and found the switch on a lamp. It had been working before, but now it didn't light. They must've turned the generator off. There was only the moonlight coming through the window. I put something on and crept to the door. It opened straight on to the living room, which was all dark of course. It was pretty quiet. There were insects or something, chirping outside.

I went to the veranda where Roo was. I could see the lumpy shadow of the pillowcase. I touched it very gently, and I could feel Roo in there. She kind of twitched a bit when I touched her. I wanted to take her out and take her to bed with me, but it seemed cruel to disturb her.

It was hotter than I'd ever dreamt it could be at night.

I decided I wanted to pee.

My boots were standing on the veranda. I put them on and went down the steps. A half-moon was shining down over the yard. It was weird how bright it was – it's never like that in London. I could see the dunny, but it looked a long way off. I went to the shade house and crouched in its shadow. Oddly enough I felt safer than in the dunny.

The redback song was going through my head. I hoped nothing would bite my bum.

As I was creeping back to bed, I suddenly stopped. There was something on the other side of the yard that I hadn't noticed before – a sort of platform. I went closer, and I got a shock. It was some big barrel-things pushed together, with boards across the top. On it was *someone asleep*. Two someones. They lay in the moonlight with just a sheet over them.

The one nearest to me was Gran. I crept round the other side. The other one was Dave.

Chapter Six

Next morning I woke up all sticky, even though I'd slept in my knickers without even a sheet. It was very early. I could smell cooking and I could hear Gran's and Dave's voices.

I dressed quickly and went through into the big room. Dave was sitting at the table. He looked up when I came in and kind of lifted his hand in a half-wave. Then he looked back down into his mug of tea. Gran came in from the kitchen with a dish of eggs. She gave me a big smile. Of course she was back to no make-up and she was wearing shorts and a sleeveless top. She still wore her boots. Her legs didn't look so good bare. Knobbly knees. What a difference from London! I still wasn't used to it.

"What would you like to eat? You can have your eggs fried, boiled, poached or scrambled."

The mere thought of a cooked breakfast nearly made me throw up. I said, "Can I have cereal?"

"Sorry, Dave's let us run out."

"I only got into town once, all the time you were *away*," he said in a grumbling voice. I guessed he'd been really lonely and fed up without her. After what I'd seen in the night, that made even more sense. "How was I to know there'd be someone wanting cereal?"

He stabbed the yolks of his eggs suddenly with his fork, one-two, as if he thought they would get him if he didn't get them first.

Gran said, "You can have plain toast and Vegemite."

Vegemite turned out to be salty brown paste, like Marmite. I smeared some on the toast and nibbled it and drank three mugs of tea. I'd never been so thirsty because I'd never sweated so much.

I kept glancing at Dave under my eyebrows. They'd been sleeping together on that platform-thing, outdoors. Talk about back to nature. I looked away. I felt just completely embarrassed even to be with them.

"Have you forgotten you've got a baby?" Gran asked, pretending to be stern.

Roo! I had forgotten! I jumped up and ran out to the porch. Roo's little head was poking out of the top of the pillowcase. She was looking at me as if to say, "Where've you been, what kind of mum are you?" I scooped her up and gave her a good cuddle, and before I could stop her, she'd dived down the front of my crop-top and fallen straight out the bottom on to the floor.

She twisted her body over and sat there looking absolutely surprised and shocked. The bottom had *really* fallen out of her world! "Oh, poor little girl!" I said. I felt so guilty. What if you dropped a real baby? I picked her up and comforted her and kissed her and went to the kitchen to get her bottle ready.

"I let her fall on the floor," I said. "Head first. Do you think she's hurt?"

Gran looked at her and rubbed her head. "They're pretty tough. She's all right."

I got on with making her bottle. Then I heard myself say, "Gran."

"What?"

"Where were you last night?"

"I made a bed out on the forty-fours."

"Forty-fours?"

"Forty-four gallon fuel drums."

I didn't say anything, just stirred the milk, but she looked at me and noticed I was blushing, maybe. Or something.

"What's wrong?"

"Is Dave your boyfriend?"

She looked at me, like, startled. But then she smiled, a very young smile, sort of twinkly. "It's a funny word to use about old codgers like us. But I suppose it about covers it." She made a clicking noise. "There's life in the old dog yet, eh?"

I really did blush now. Only because they were old, obviously. It is so *gross* thinking about old people doing it. It's bad enough with parents, never mind *grand*parents. But I decided to act cool. I cleared my throat. "And do you always sleep out in the summer?"

"Yeah, unless there's a dust storm. If you like, you can sleep outside, too, on my shearer's bed."

"No thanks," I said. On the "forty-fours" you'd be safe from snakes, but you wouldn't on that low camp bed. I didn't say any more. I thought Gran should at least have been a bit embarrassed, or ashamed, or *something*. I once walked into Dad and Mum's bedroom and caught them at it. Neither of them could look me in the eye for a week.

After I'd fed Roo I was depressed and sweaty and I really needed a shower. I decided not to ask Gran to go up on the roof for me again. The ladder was still there so I took the plastic bottle across the yard to the bath tub under the windmill. I felt the water. It *was* cooler than the air. If only Dave hadn't been around I'd have stripped off and got in, but he was.

115

I lugged two bottles of water across the yard and up on to the roof of the wash house (the weight! You wouldn't believe!). All that work nearly did for me. I was knackered, even though I'd left Roo out of my "pouch". She hopped around after me looking pathetic, but I had to be hardhearted. I suppose mums often have to, I mean you can only stand so much.

I went into the wash house, stripped off and turned on the tap. The water came down in a solid stream, muggy warm, same temperature as the air. After all that effort, it didn't cool me, it didn't refresh me. There was no escape from the heat. I felt trapped.

And, maybe because I was in a bad mood anyway, I sort of lost it. What was I doing here? What had Gran been thinking of to drag me thousands and thousands of miles from home to this hellish hot place with no proper *nothing*? She wanted to give me a good time! Yeah, right. Some good time this was.

Standing under that so-called shower I started counting the days till I could go home. And that made me start subtracting the number of days I'd already been away.

Suddenly I froze. Not cold-froze (worse luck) – moving-froze. I stood there with my mouth open and the water running into it. Wait a minute! I tried to work it out but the days sort of blurred. Left London the evening of the

116

eighteenth… arrived the nineteenth, no, you go *forward* in time going east, the twentieth… two full days in Perth, or was it three, that brought it to the twenty-third… a day and a night on the road… then last night – yes! Today must be the twenty-fifth! The twenty-fifth of December!

Just at that moment I felt something like a cheese grater scraping against my back.

I ricked my neck, looking quickly over my shoulder, and got the fright of my life. There was this great shaggy head sticking through the little window, with a huge pink tongue about a mile long reaching for my skin!

I screamed and jumped back against the wet wall, knocking my head. Some other poisoning Aussie monster was trying to bite me!

I was so scared! I was out of the wash house in one second. I ran right through the house and across the veranda, scattering drops of water, without a stitch on me. As I burst out of the front door and jumped down the steps, I saw Gran standing by the ute. Dave was there too. He took one look over his shoulder at me flying towards them like a flasher. I saw his mouth drop open, and then— I don't know where he went, he just wasn't there any more.

By the time I reached Gran she was laughing so hard she nearly fell over. She grabbed me the minute I hurled myself on her and bundled me into the ute cabin. I was all, like, out of breath and half sobbing.

"Gran, Gran, there's a big woolly *thing* trying to kill me!"

She was weak from laughing. She closed the door on me and leant against the ute, wiping her eyes. She made a bleating noise like a sheep when she spoke. "Poor Stace! Is that it?" And she pointed back at the house.

Round the side of it came this big shambling furry thing.

Gran ran over to it and patted its face. "Poor Humpy! Did Stacey frighten you? Come and meet her, she's all right really." She put her arm round its neck and brought it over to the ute. "Meet Humpy White," she said. "He's a sweetie. He was probably just trying to get a drink from your shower."

Of course now I could see all of it, I saw what it was. It was a baby camel.

I felt such a total idiot. I put my wet head down on the steering wheel. My heart was pounding. Dave had seen me in the raw. I felt *humiliated*. I wanted to scream. God I hated this mad place!

"Come on, stroke him. You gave him a fright, too, you know."

I didn't move. She took my limp hand through the ute window, and next thing I felt this soft fur and some rubbery lips kind of nibbling my hand. I peeped sideways. The monster-head was just a baby camel's head now, and, yes, he was rather sweet with his long eyelashes and soft mouth with the top lip kind of split in two. But I wasn't going to give in. I snatched my hand away.

"He's not white," I said. "Stupid great ugly thing."

"Well, he's whiter than a grown-up camel," said Gran reasonably. "You OK? Out you get then. I'm off to check a windmill."

I lost it again and shouted, "Sod the rotten windmill, Gran! It's Christmas Day!"

She looked a bit startled. "Oh, is it? Hey, you could be right. Happy Christmas. D'you want to come? Here, stick this jacket on and go get into your gear."

"I don't want to meet Dave," I muttered, nearly crying.

"Dave won't say a word, don't worry! He'll act like he didn't see you."

I skulked into the house like a criminal. Luckily I didn't meet him on my way through to get my clothes and collect Roo. But he had seen me. That was one reason why I went with Gran, because after that little episode I was dead embarrassed to be left alone with him.

Besides, I needed a major, *major* sulk. I was livid with Gran and I wanted her to feel it, so I had to go with her, otherwise I might've been over it by the time she came back.

I was totally silent as we drove along, bumping over the rough track. *"Happy Christmas, let's go and check a windmill."*

119

I *ask* you. She hadn't even noticed it was Christmas! I'd never heard of a place in the *entire world* where they don't make a special fuss of Christmas Day!

Whatever you can say about my mum, she's very good at Christmas. However skint we were, it was always special. She'd dig out the old plastic tree and press down the branches (they kind of fold up to pack away) and we'd decorate it with the baubles and stuff that we've always had – I think they must've been Nan's, they were very old ones, the angel was a doll made of celluloid (pre-plastic stuff, not nearly so strong, her face was all cracked and one arm had fallen off), she was definitely Nan's when she was young – she was a bit naff with her old silver dress going green, but she had tinsel wings and a wire to fix her to the top of the tree. I used to call her Samantha, which I thought of as a really posh name (why I thought angels would be posh, I don't know). The fairy lights packed up years ago and last year I'd saved up and bought a new string. That really made a difference, the way they shone on the glass balls and tinsel.

And there were always presents, usually something like a little bag of skin-stuff for Mum and a CD for me, and a proper sit-down-at-the-table dinner in the living room, which normally we never do, it's just TV dinners or eating at the breakfast bar in the kitchen. Mum insisted on a turkey, even though it's neither of our favourite meat, for tradition. She'd buy the smallest size you can get (frozen) and do it with lots of roasties and peas and a little round Christmas pudding that she'd turn off all the lights and set fire to with a miniature bottle of brandy. We'd have it with custard. Nan'd come round and we'd give her our presents and she'd talk about Grandpa and get a bit weepy and slurry voiced on the half-bottle of port she always brought (for us, only neither of us like port so Nan had to drink it all). There was nearly always a row or a mood, or a bit of snapping from one of us (especially before Dad left) but that didn't last and it was all part of it.

And suddenly I wanted it, all of it. And Grandma Glendine had done me out of it. She'd even done me out of the right grey, wintry, Christmassy weather.

It meant she hadn't got me a present or anything, and needless to say, no turkey. Where would anyone get a turkey in this wilderness? We'd probably have fried eggs for Christmas dinner – no, Christmas tea! And what if Mum had come home and she and Nan were sitting there all miserable because I wasn't there to do Christmas for? I just wanted to crawl away somewhere and cry my eyes out. Roo, in my shirt, seemed to feel my bad mood and curled up and went to sleep to get away from it.

After for ever, I realised Gran wasn't even noticing my sulk. She was cracking her gum and humming under her breath, all cheerful – the redback song, wasn't it? "Stace," she said casually, "can you find my shades, I think I dropped them behind the seat."

I got on my knees to face backwards. The sunglasses were on a kind of ledge. And then I saw something else. It was a *gun*. A real gun, a rifle or something like one. It was stuck into a kind of holder-thing that was fixed to the back wall of the cabin.

"What's that?" I pointed.

"What does it look like?"

"But what's it for?"

"It – is – for – *shooting* things," she said, very slowly, like I was a duck-brain.

"What d'you shoot?" I kind of croaked.

"Roo, mostly."

I couldn't believe I was hearing this. My hands clutched my Roo. "You kill kangaroos? On purpose?"

"We shoot them for meat sometimes when we run out and haven't time to go into town."

I was *speechless*. All my anger rushed back. How could she shoot a beautiful kangaroo?

"And bush turkeys," she added after a long silence.

I sat up and looked at her. "Turkeys? Like for..."

"For Christmas. Yeah. Too bad we're not likely to see one. If we did, maybe you could have the kind of Christmas

122

dinner you're used to." She gave me a quick glance. "Mind you, they're a protected species. I could go to jail for shooting one. Would you help me pluck and gut it? I hate that job."

I made a face but she didn't see it. Was it worth it? First to shoot it, then to pull its feathers off and take its guts out? No, it definitely wasn't.

"Don't let's bother, Gran," I said, kind of sarky, but she didn't get it.

We bumped over a bit of a rise, and suddenly—

"There they are!" Gran shouted. "See them?"

I half stood up. There they were, maybe twenty silver-grey cows, in a dip right ahead. They were all crowding round near a windmill. I saw it was turning all right, but Gran said, "When they're all just hanging around like that, it means there's no water."

"Is Spotty there?"

Gran leant out of the window as she drove nearer. "Yes, there she is! See, that smaller one with the white spot on her face? Hey, she's grown! Hi there, Spotty!" She braked as we got near to the cows. I was just going to get out when I saw something scary. Two of them, that were bigger than the others, squared up to each other looking as if they wanted to fight. They lowered their heads and started pushing each other.

"I didn't know cows fought," I said. Gran roared with laughter.

"Don't you know a cow from a bull?" she said. "Maybe I better give you some lessons in anatomy!"

She jumped out and went straight to a trough-thing. "Bone dry," she called. "See? I told you."

Now I saw that between the windmill and the cattle was a weird sort of mass of junk that made a fence. It was all wired together somehow or stuck into the ground. It wouldn't have kept out anything cleverer than a cow. Gran found a sort of gate. Not a real gate, of course, just an iron bed-spring lying on its side, wired to a couple of posts made of pipes.

"Come and lend a hand with this!" she called.

I clocked the bulls, but they weren't bothered about me, they were glaring at each other and pawing the ground. I kind of crept out (leaving Roo safely asleep), slithered round to the safe side of the ute and helped Gran heave this old bed-spring gate out of the way so we could get to the windmill.

Next to the windmill was a tank. There was a pipe leading from it to the trough on the other side of the fence. The tank was empty, and I could see why – the pipe that went down into the ground was leaking. As the windmill spun round in the breeze, there was a sort of thunking noise and the pipe gushed out water from a split in its side. It just ran down the hole by the pipe, instead of going into the tank.

Gran said, "OK, Stace, we have to mend this."

"How?"

"It's got a cut from the brass coupling inside it rubbing a hole in it. So we have to put a bandage on."

"A *bandage!*"

"A rubber one."

She led the way to the ute. The back of it was full of all kinds of junk – bits of rope, tin, wood, pipes, a saucepan, and other odds and ends that could have been almost anything. There was even an old scrubbing brush. Gran pulled a cardboard box towards her and I saw it was full of shiny black things like a whale's intestines. When I picked one up, I could see it was the inner tube from a car tyre.

She got a big pair of scissors out of the box of junk. "Here, you can cut the bandage," she said. "Cut right around the tube, longways. Make it about two inches wide."

"How many centimetres is two inches?"

"Don't ask me. About this wide," and she held out her finger and thumb.

She left me to it. I dug the point of the scissors through the rubber and worked one blade in and then started trying to cut. It was impossible! I had to really struggle to cut even a little bit. It took me ages and my hand got well tired and sore. At last Gran came back and found me nearly crying with frustration.

"I can't do it, Gran!"

She took it away from me and in about two seconds she'd finished it and cut the end square. "Now roll it, like a nurse rolls a real bandage," she said.

Well, I could do that all right. Gran cut two more lengths, and I rolled those too. Gran was clipping some bits of wire out of that so-called fence.

"Come on, Stace, now we mend the pipe."

She took my first bandage and wrapped it tight around the leaky part of the pipe. Then she twisted the wires to hold it in place. She had some pliers to tighten the ends. Then she did it again. I was handing her things like a nurse in a hospital while the doctor operates. As soon as she'd finished, water started to go into the tank, a little at a time. Splosh, splosh, splosh. It was a nice, satisfying sound.

"When the tank fills up a bit, it'll start running down that other pipe into the trough," Gran said. "Then my little cows will get a lovely drink." She put her arm across my shoulders in a pally way, as if we'd done something amazing together.

Suddenly she lifted her arm off me and sprinted up a ladder that was fixed to the windmill. She was looking out across the bush. I looked where she was looking and I saw a cloud of red dust quite a long way off. I couldn't see what was making it – it looked like a squirrel with a red bushy tail running along the horizon.

"Come on, Stacey, we must get back," Gran said.

She made it sound urgent. I started throwing the scissors and bits of tube back in the ute, while Gran dragged the "gate" shut and went straight to the driver's seat.

"C'mon, hurry it up!" she said, impatient, sticking her head out the window.

"What's wrong?"

"Nothing. Looks like visitors. Let's get back."

"Is it the Wonngais?" I asked. I felt excited. "Maybe it's Merinda, come to visit me!"

"Maybe," Gran said.

Chapter Seven

I'd completely forgotten about my Christmas sulk. But maybe she hadn't, because halfway there, she suddenly skidded to a stop. She was staring off to the right. I followed her eyes but I couldn't see anything, just the bits of bush and the rocky ground.

"Speak of the devil!"

"What is it, Gran?"

"Give me the gun, Stace," she said quietly.

I knelt up and pulled the rifle out of its holder. If it had been red hot, I couldn't have liked touching it less. I handed it to her.

She took the gun from me and rested it on the windowsill on her side.

"Now give me a bullet out of the glove box."

She was talking so quietly that I found myself opening the compartment door without a sound. There were the bullets, just lying there. I gave her one. She fitted it into the gun. Then she put her face down close to the wooden part and she was absolutely still for a few seconds. I had a funny, mixed-up feeling. Of course I didn't want her to shoot anything, but I was excited too.

There was a huge bang. I was expecting it, but still it made me jump. The gun jumped, too, and I saw a sudden movement about twenty metres from the ute. Something big had sprung up out of the grass and fallen back.

"Got him!" she said.

"What? What?"

She didn't answer. She thrust the gun at me and jumped out and started running through the bush. When she reached the place where I'd seen the movement, she bent down and picked something up. It was a big bird. I thought it was a baby emu for a minute! And it was stone dead.

She came back holding it by the feet. She was well pleased with herself.

"Here's your Christmas turkey, Stacey!" she said. "See? I took his hat off!" Half its head was gone.

She reached in and put it on the floor at my feet. I looked at it as we drove on. It had been alive ten minutes ago and now it was dead and we were going to pluck it and gut it. And cook it and eat it. I shuddered. I was disgusted. And Gran guessed my thoughts, because she laughed and said, "What's your problem? Just because it usually comes from the supermarket all oven-ready!" Which was true. They all have to be killed some way or other, probably a worse way than being shot.

We drove into the homestead yard. The "squirrel" I'd seen was a motorbike. It was a huge one – a Harley Davidson, I think, a two-seater. It would've been all shiny with its chrome fittings, if it hadn't been thick with red dust. I felt Gran relax beside me.

"Well, it isn't the mob this time."

"The mob? You mean the Aborigines?"

"Yeah, but it isn't them. It's some tourists. What's the betting they're lost and run out of petrol? Or maybe they set off without hats and they've got sunstroke, that'd be typical!"

I was disappointed it wasn't Merinda. But anyway it was someone from the outside world at least. We went into the house, and there they were, two American young men. They did have hats – well, helmets. But she was right about them being lost. They were looking for a town called Cosmo Newberry, an Aboriginal township they said, where they were going to try to buy some artefacts.

"Preferably like this," one said.

I saw they were looking at a huge dark-coloured egg. I thought it must be the emu one Gran had told me about, that she hadn't got around to showing me. Dave had got it out for them. He was standing there looking hopeful. Over the heads of the bikers, he gave Gran some eye signals that Mum would've been proud of. I read it as, *Maybe they'll buy it!* Gran got the same message and moved in like lightning. She almost snatched it out of their hands.

"Oh, they've got plenty like that in the shop in Cosmo," she said.

"This one's beautiful. Is it for sale?" said one of the bikers.

"Yes," said Dave, but Gran spoke over him.

"No it's not. Sorry." She handed it to me, as if for safe keeping.

The second I had my hands on it, I wanted it. I *really* wanted it! It was well beautiful. The most beautiful artefact I'd ever seen. It was about six inches tall (I could just imagine a tiny emu curled up in it) and this really incredible colour, a wonderful dark blue-green, like nothing else I could think of. Like a new colour, sort of sea and forest mixed. A picture was scratched into the surface, through to where the shell was white. It was an oval frame shape with a lovely picture in it of a kangaroo standing among some Aboriginal boys. It was *brilliant*. It had a little stand that went with it, so you could stand it up. Gran handed me that, too.

131

"Hey, are you sure you don't want to sell it?" asked the other biker. "I'd pay top dollar for it – it's amazing."

"I'm sorry," said Gran shortly.

"Awww…"

"I'm giving it to my granddaughter." My head came up and my mouth dropped open. "It's her Christmas present. Happy Christmas, Stacey," she said, and gave me a kiss.

It was too late for the bikers (or "bikies" as Dave and Gran called them) to get to Cosmo Newberry that evening, so they stayed over the night. And it was good they did, because guess who had to do the plucking and gutting? She set them to work behind the wash house. All I had to do was watch. What I watched wasn't the poor turkey (which was actually called an Australian bustard) it was them, and if I hadn't been so thankful it wasn't me, I'd have had a good laugh.

They had fun at first, making gobbling noises and flinging feathers in all directions, but when they got down to reaching their hands up its *backside* into its innards and pulling out all this urky stuff, it was something else! They started hauling, like, *miles* of some grey tubing out. It was *totally* gross, and made the most revolting stink. Gran had to finish the job because they both turned green and went skulking off, saying they had to throw up.

"Wimps," she whispered to me. "I wouldn't have rescued them, except if they'd bust the gall bladder they'd have ruined it." But I was so grateful to them for being there, otherwise it would have been me nearly passing out from the stench off all those yucky innards.

We had an amazing Christmas dinner. Dave and Gran cut up the bustard into big joints and wrapped them in layers and layers of foil (I helped) and cooked them in a fire-pit outdoors. It took ages, but it was worth the wait. The bikies, whose names were Scott and Jeffrey, did all the hard work, collecting wood and keeping the fire going. We had one big laugh, because Gran forgot to tell them about kicking the wood first and a snake was there!

Poor Jeff got the fright of his life when it slithered out. He threw a branch at it and swore his head off, and ran one way, while the snake ran the other, more scared than he was. It shot out of the yard like an arrow and away into the bush before Gran could shoot it, only she said she wouldn't have anyway. She said she only shoots snakes when they're in the house.

But she told them it was a deadly poisonous one and they were both white as ghosts. And suddenly I realised that I'd jumped up to see it better, I hadn't been scared of it a bit. But the bikies had the wind up them, and after going into a huddle they said, "Can snakes climb up barrels?"

Gran and Dave roared with laughter. "D'you want to sleep in our bed?"

"Well, if there might be snakes in the house..."

Gran said OK, and winked at me. "We're not afraid of snakes in the house, are we, Stace?" I knew there weren't any really, in spite of the dugite. That was a one-off.

We sat out as the sun went down. The fire-pit (which had foil-wrapped potatoes in it too) glowed and Dave dished out beer and Coke and we all got hungrier and hungrier. We sang carols and then Dave started to tell a dirty story, but Gran shut him up quick and said we should all tell about our favourite Christmases.

Scott's was when he was ten years old and his parents took him to Disneyland. Gran's was the last one she'd had before my dad bombed off to England, when he'd taken her out for a special Christmas dinner at a restaurant in Melbourne with his own money and she hadn't had to do any cooking. I liked that one because my dad did something really nice in it. Dave's was when he was on board a cruise ship as a steward (he'd done loads of different jobs in his life) and the chief steward, who was in charge of them, wasn't there for some reason, so after they'd served Christmas dinner to the passengers, they'd sat down in the dining room and eaten all the same fantastic food the punters had had, and drank what was left in all their glasses and got totally smashed. Mine was what I've described, pretty well every Christmas I remember.

Jeff kept very quiet.

"What about you, Jeff?" I asked. Tact, eh? Should've known there was something wrong.

He said, "I was brung up in a home. Every Christmas was the same and it wasn't too great. They did their best, I guess, but it was always sort of impersonal." Then he looked at the ground and muttered, "I think this is about the best Christmas I ever had so far."

None of us said anything, and then Gran put her hand on his knee. "You've got lots to come," she said. "You just wait and see."

And the rest of us said, "Yaaay, Jeff!" and that well cheered him up.

At last the bush turkey was cooked and Dave dug it out and unwrapped it. It was a bit tough, but still it was wonderful. We sort of tore it to pieces between us with whoops of hunger and threw the bones over our shoulders like Henry the Eighth. I wasn't scared of dingoes coming any more – I sort of wished they would, I'd've liked to see one. We were all laughing and the bikies and Dave and even Gran were a bit pissed and we were kind of crazy from having a good time and stuffing our faces with this delicious meat.

The moon came up at last and we were still there in the firelight, singing and talking. The bikies were very sweet to Roo and petted her and tried to feed her titbits. She hopped from one to the other like a little dog. But she always came back to me. When she was tired she jumped into my shirt. The bikies thought that was the most fantastic thing they'd ever seen in their lives and wanted her to do it again like a trick, but of course I wasn't having that. She wasn't a sideshow. I only let them take two photos of her peeping out of my top, because I thought the flash would frighten her.

When at last it was time to turn in, the bikies had a wild time heaving themselves up on the forty-fours and pushing each other off (they were pretty far gone by then). Gran called out, "Goodnight, sleep tight, mind the snakes don't bite!" Then us three trooped into the house. I kissed Roo and put her to bed in her pillowcase and then Gran and I kissed each other goodnight.

"Not such a bad old Christmas after all, eh, Stace?"

I didn't ask if she'd have remembered if I hadn't. I said, "The food was delicious, and my emu egg is my best present ever." That made me feel a bit disloyal because Mum and Nan always bought me the best presents they could.

I think Gran guessed what I was thinking because she said, "I'm sorry I couldn't give you what you *really* wanted most, lovie. I just bet they're missing you, both of them, wherever they are, the m—" But she didn't say it.

I set my emu egg up on my table. In the moonlight it looked mysterious. The picture stood out, white against dark, like a tiny scene that I could see from my bed. It *was* my best-ever present. And as I dropped off, I thought that even though I wasn't Jeff, who'd always had rotten Christmases, this had certainly been my most interesting one.

Chapter Eight

The days started to go by quickly after the bikies left. It felt a bit lonely without them. But there was always something to do during the day and I started enjoying it. I couldn't hate it any more, not after that special Christmas which was really *unique*.

I won't say I got used to the heat or the flies, but what was the use of moaning about it? I stopped minding about sweating, in fact it was good. When you sweat you can feel the tiniest little breeze on your skin. When I was outside I held my arms away from my body so the air could cool under them. I tied back my hair, but the hair band made my head even hotter, so I asked Gran to cut it. She cut it short all over my head and I gave a scream when I saw it, but luckily it's very curly so after a wash (and with some wax rubbed into it) it looked all right, nice and spiky. It was a lot cooler. The downside was, Dave kept teasing me. He said it looked like feathers and he started calling me chook.

I fed the real chooks and collected the eggs, which was OK, I wasn't scared any more. I was a bit more scared of the emus because they were so big. I betted they could give you a really hefty peck with those big beaks. But Nora and Dora were so sweet, they never pecked. I had to give them lots of oats and chook-pellets and scraps, and they gobbled it up, you could almost see them getting fat on it.

Humpy White came around a lot and he and Roo got friendly. Roo would hop over to Humpy and look up at him and he'd bend his head down and sniff at Roo and sometimes he pushed her over. I worried about Humpy being too big and too rough, but Gran said they were only young creatures playing and they wouldn't hurt each other.

The problem was the evenings.

When I was about eight, my dad read me *Charlie and the Chocolate Factory*. It was the first book I remember really liking. In that book the writer wrote a poem about what kids would do if there was no TV. He said they'd read. In fact I think he said they'd read and read and read and read. Well, I proved him wrong on that one.

The evenings were *awful*. My worst time, the time I got bored and homesick. I just didn't know what to do with myself. Oh, there were books, quite a few, and Gran kept telling me I should read (not that she did, she was banging away at her computer every spare minute). Dave didn't read, he just lay about and swigged beer from the can and listened to the radio or his tapes, playing Australian music. He was crazy about someone called Slim Dusty who sang really twangy outbacky kind of songs about cattle-camp and railways and stuff, and the old days. Dave never played any proper pop and it really got on my *wick*. I started hating the radio, just because it wasn't TV.

So at first I just slumped around every night and went to bed early.

Some nights Gran would lay off her computer for ten minutes and talk to me to keep me company, but not very often. One night when I was especially bored, I went right into her bedroom where the computer was and asked her, "Gran. Why do you live out here? I mean, you seemed such a city kind of person in London."

She stopped tapping away and turned around. I saw she was smoking. She hastily stubbed out her cigarette. "Sorry, Stace," she said. "That's why I chew all that gum, because I'm trying hard to give up, but when I'm writing it's kind of a habit." Then she said, "I don't know if your dad mentioned it, but *his* dad nicked off, too."

140

"Did what?" I asked. (Stupid. I got it a second too late.)

"Vamoosed. Ran away. Dumped me. So then I was alone for a few of years. I was still pretty young. Me and your dad – he was just a kid then, about fifteen – we moved to Melbourne. I abandoned this place, sold the cattle and hopped it. Life's no joke out here on your own with a kid. Especially one who doesn't help too much."

"What happened to your first husband?"

"Who? No, no, your grandpa was my first. The other one was my second, *after* your grandpa. Real hotshot city type. We met at a party and were married within a month. He moved me into his house in Melbourne, and I thought I'd died and gone to heaven. But after only about a year, that's just what *he* did."

Well, that explained how she got so rich. Naturally it wouldn't be my dad who had a dad who could buy big houses with three TVs and leave a lot of money. Genes count for *something*.

"So we lived in the Melbourne house till your dad was old enough to go away to uni, only he dropped out after the first six weeks, the lazy mongrel, and he nicked off to pommy-land and met your mum. I haven't seen hide nor hair of him since then, just the odd letter or postcard, usually wanting money. And that's fifteen years back, no, sixteen it must be.

"After he went, I tried to settle back to the single life in Melbourne but – well, let's just say things got a bit sticky. I was lonely and I started to miss the bush. Maybe you think that's strange. I can be a city person, like you said – I like living it up, dressing to kill in my slipperies and shinies, but there's this other side to me. The down to earth side that I was born to. My dad owned this place. I lived here till I was thirty-three. This crazy life's in my blood.

"So I came back here. I was tough and healthy in those days, and I thought I could manage on my own, but it was harder than I expected. Lonely, too.

"One time the mob came through. Usually they're OK, I get along fine with 'em, but that time some of them had been on the grog and I got scared. One of them was chasing his wife with a machete and she ran into my kitchen and he came after her—"

"Gran! What'd you do?"

"Oh, I calmed him down and got the machete off him, but I was really shaken up. I'd just painted the kitchen white and I thought it was going to get blood splattered all up the walls."

"Not to mention the poor wife getting killed!"

"Oh yeah, that too. I thought, enough's enough. And just about after that, Dave came through on his motorbike. He was between jobs, and I had a few for him to do, and

142

somehow… he just stayed. He's been with me for ten years. More use to me than either of my husbands, I'll tell you that."

But there weren't many interesting conversations like that. So I had nothing to do but play with Roo and sit, and think. I imagined Gran living it up in a big house, part of the social scene, and then running back to her roots because the city was *lonely*. Lonely – compared to this? What about all her friends – she must've had some if she went to parties?

And there was another puzzle. If Dad had been knocking on her door for money, why hadn't she ever sent him any? I'd already found out that calling your son a mongrel might not be exactly a compliment, but it didn't mean you hated them. Disappointed with them, yes, fed up they'd bombed off and left you, but if you were rich and they were poor *and* had a family, I mean, you'd help them, wouldn't you? There was nothing tightfisted about Gran Glendine. She was generous, like it was in her nature. I just couldn't figure it out.

Any more than I'd ever been able to figure out my parents.

Mum's a worker, I'll give her that. Working at the checkout in Safeways isn't a job I'd do unless I was starving, but it keeps us, kind of. So I had to admire her for sticking at it. But it didn't make me think she had much brain, until one day I asked her why she didn't get bored.

"I like it," she said. "Always different faces, I can make up stories about them. And then it's fun, seeing what they buy. I can work out a lot about them from that, whether they're on health-kicks, or hard up, or dieting, or got a big family, or a party coming up. I can even tell if they're a bit posh without hearing them speak, just by looking at their shopping. And that's before they've bought newspapers," she added seriously. "Of course if they've bought a paper it's a dead giveaway, I don't count that."

I'd stared at her. First-off it seemed barmy, but then I thought, something *is* going on in her head after all. I'd be, like, dying of boredom, but she'd made quite a complicated game out of the job that I'd never've thought of.

Then there's Dad. What a loser. What a *dosser*. And he didn't need to be. He had a chance to go to "uni". (Of course I'd guessed that's university.) Dropped out, of course he did! Made for each other, those two. Well, at least my mum had some sense of responsibility. *She'd* never run out on me.

Oh.

Well, but that wasn't exactly running out. Not permanently, no matter what Gran said. Gran was just cynical, because of what'd happened to her. Mum'd come back. Of course she would. Dad might be a priority, because he was in trouble and she was nuts about him. But I was her only child. That had to count for *something*.

* * *

A few days after Christmas, when I went into the feed store to get some grain for the chooks and emus, I caught sight of something flickering away as I opened the door. I screamed cos I knew it was a snake. I ran to tell Gran. She said, "We need a goanna." So we went hunting one.

That was a fun day. We drove around for hours. We never saw one, but we did see lots of different birds, a couple of snakes and some of Roo's relations (in the distance, luckily – I didn't trust Gran not to shoot one, we'd run out of meat and Dave was complaining). Just as the sun was setting and we were heading back, Gran let out a shout and put the brake on and pointed.

There on the road was a little creature so crazy looking that I just didn't believe it could be real. If a mini-monster can be beautiful, it was. It wasn't a goanna, but it *was* a kind of lizard. It had gold and black patches on its skin and weird-looking spikes sticking out all over it including on its head. I was just amazed and couldn't even breathe while we watched it sort of waddle-scuttling across the road.

"That's a thorny devil," Gran said. "Aren't they something? Like tiny dinosaurs! But they're no good for catching snakes."

"You ought to get a dog," I said.

"No more dogs. I can't bear to lose another."

"Did they all die?"

"Yeah. They will go for snakes and the snakes kill them. One got run over. Another got poisoned with the strychnine bait the government fella puts down for dingoes. I've given up on dogs, you love 'em too much."

"More than the emus?"

"Mmm. Not that I don't love Nora and Dora. But they don't sleep on your bed. Or bark when the mob comes through."

Dave was drinking too much. This got on Gran's nerves, and she nagged him. It reminded me of Mum and Dad, arguing about him boozing. It didn't put me off Dave, because he did something fantastic for me. He taught me to drive the ute.

When he first suggested it I didn't believe he meant it. I thought he was teasing. But he wasn't.

"You never know when you might need to," he said.

"But aren't I too young?"

"Young! You're fourteen, aren't you? Most kids in the bush learn to drive when they're twelve. Of course you can't drive on the highway, but out here who's to know?"

First he drove me out to a big cleared strip that I hadn't seen before.

"What's this?" I asked. "It looks like a place for planes to land."

"Maybe cos that's just what it is."

"You mean it's an airfield?"

"Yeah, it's where the Flying Doctors would come in, if we needed them. Now, change places."

He sat me in the driver's seat and got in again beside me.

"Now then," he said, "turn on the engine. Good, you knew how to do that. Now, put your right foot on the brake pedal – that's the one in the middle. That's the same foot you use on the accelerator – the one on the right. That's what'll make it go forward, it's what makes the engine rev. Try it – go on, it's safe, we're on the flat and you're not in gear."

I pushed down a bit on the right pedal and the engine roared. Wow. It was like a wild lion wanting to pounce. I could feel its power and it was exciting.

"OK," said Dave. "Now what you do is, you keep your right foot on the brake and put your left foot on the clutch pedal."

He showed me how to engage the gear stick in first gear and let the clutch up slowly.

"Atta girl, good, you're off!"

And I was! The ute moved forward. I was driving!

It was very jerky at first because my left foot wouldn't

come up smoothly, and then when I felt the ute beginning to *really* go, I panicked and took my right foot off the accelerator. The ute made a horrible noise and kind of jumped to a stop.

Dave laughed. "You've stalled it. Never mind. Turn on the ignition and try again. Don't be scared. When you want to stop, put both feet down hard – one on the clutch and one on the brake. You can't brake and rev up at the same time, so it always stops, but you have to disengage the gear or you stall."

Dave told me I was catching on "real quick". Soon I was driving – slowly – down the airstrip. After a bit I got more confidence and I could go a bit faster and get into second gear. I had to slow down to do the turn each time. After about twenty minutes I got braver, I went up to 30 k an hour and got into third gear!

I was so excited I could hardly wait to rush into the house when we got back, and tell Gran I could drive! I jumped around until I saw Roo was a bit scared, and then I did a dance of pride. I was so thrilled that when Dave came strolling into the house after me, I rushed up to him and gave him a hug. He was just hugging me back, when I said, "I can't wait to get home and tell everyone I can drive!"

Dave dropped his arms and turned away very suddenly.

* * *

That night Dave downed about six cans of Emu Bitters and got really pissed. When Gran gave him curry he got the sulks (I remembered Dad doing that too) so I felt uncomfortable and went to bed early. I could still hear them arguing through the window, even after they'd gone to bed (to forty-four gallon drums, I should say). I heard my name once or twice. Could it be anything to do with me being here that had set him off? Maybe he wanted me to go home. But I'd stopped being homesick after Christmas Day. I wasn't counting the days any more. Unless maybe I was counting how many I had left.

I hadn't stopped thinking about Mum and Dad though, wondering where they were and what was happening. It was sort of awful, being so cut off. But in another way I loved it. A bit like being dead, maybe. I know that sounds funny. But I often think what Nan said when Grandpa died. She cried a lot but then she blew her nose and said, "Well, he's out of it. Nothing can hurt him or touch him now." I was where nothing to do with my real life could hurt or touch me (so I thought) and I don't deny it – at the time that suited me fine.

After that, I had a driving lesson every day. When I got more confident I begged Dave to let me go on the big main road. There was absolutely no traffic at all and it was so tempting, dead straight and empty, what could happen? I nagged him till he gave in. It was really amazing. I went into top gear and drove at 60 k – that's about forty miles an hour! Dave made me do emergency stops and then he taught me how to reverse and how to turn. Of course on that big wide road you could've done a U-turn with a London bus, so I didn't have to do a proper three-point turn like you have to to pass your driving test. But I didn't care. I thought I was getting well good, I mean I was really driving.

But then, as we were zooming along, I actually saw something else on the road. It was a big piece of digging machinery bouncing along very slowly, coming the other way. I panicked and said, "Let's change places!" but Dave said, no, just to keep driving straight ahead and give the other driver a little nod as if nothing was wrong. So I did. The old guy driving gave me a bit of a funny look, I thought, but maybe that was just my conscience.

"Where's he going?" I asked. I always thought of our station being, like, at the end of everything. But the road did go on past our place.

"Probably works for the mining company."

"What mining company? A gold mine?"

"It will be. They're just exploring now."

"Is there a lot of gold around here?"

"So they say."

150

"Under our station, too?"

Dave gave me a quick look. "Yeah, maybe," he said.

"Why don't you dig it up?"

He didn't answer at once. "I worked in the mines for a while," he said. "But I got fed up with it. Maybe if it was your own mine, but sweating your guts out working for some big company – naaah. For what? To make the mine owners rich! Gouging the bush into holes, just to get a hundred thousand ounces of the yellow stuff out of the ground—"

"A hundred thousand ounces!" I didn't know what an ounce was, but it sounded a lot.

"Oh sure. That's what we'd get out of the Sons of Gwalia mine in Leonora every year. Enough to fill a bathtub. But you should see that mine. A great crater in the earth. Looks like a meteor struck. Those buggers better not show their greedy faces around here. I know 'em. I'd see 'em off."

I'd always thought Gran wasn't much hung up on rules. After all, she'd lie down in airplanes, she broke speed limits, and she'd shot our Christmas bustard, which she said you could go to jail for. But when I told her I'd driven on the road she gave Dave *more* curry. I escaped to the yard till things calmed down and played with the emus.

They knew me now and came running up to me. I must say I loved having animals do that, you know, kind of recognise you and love you, even if it was just for food. Gran had called them Nora and Dora, but I had different names for them – I called them Merinda and Loretta because of their pretty faces – I thought they needed more glamorous names. I thought of Merinda as my Wonngai friend though I never expected to see her again.

After lunch on New Year's Eve, Dave and Gran decided we had to go into town for stores.

"We're getting a bit low on fuel. And Dave's gone right through the beer," she added, giving him a bit of a dirty look, which he ignored.

I thought going into Laverton would be fun and I was ready to kill for a swim.

"Do you think we might meet Merinda?"

"I doubt it. They weren't town girls. Sorry, Stacey, I know you're short of mates out here. Tell you what, though. We'll camp overnight near the pit and I'll show you how to catch yabbies."

"What's the pit? What are yabbies?"

"You'll see."

We loaded the ute with camping gear, and were just going to set off when another ute, that made ours look practically new, drove into the yard. This time it *was* the mob! I rushed out to see them. There were loads of them,

152

men, women and kids, four crammed into the cabin and the rest in the back. They were dressed in all kinds of clothes and colours, covered with red dust. I just stood there staring until Gran gave me a hard nudge.

"What can I do for you fellas?" she asked.

The kids were staring at me. One young man who was standing up in the back, looking over the cabin, jumped over the side very gracefully, like a cat, and stood there leaning against the truck. He didn't look at me but I couldn't help looking at him. He was very handsome with his muscly dark-brown arms and legs and his masses of curly hair. I betted he'd have nice teeth if he smiled.

The driver, who was quite old, with red mud in his grey hair, got out and said, "You radio for Flying Doctor, Auntie. Wombley he got speared, he bleedin' properly."

"What he got speared for?" asked Gran, talking like them.

The older man shrugged. "Payback," he said.

"Oh. Well, get him out and let's have a look at his leg. Can he walk?"

They dropped the back of their ute and I saw a man lying there in the middle of all the others. They helped him sit up. The top of his leg was wrapped in a cloth and the cloth was, like, *soaked* with blood. He looked really weak. Gran sucked in her breath. "Looks bad. Don't move him, just let

153

him lay there. He needs a clean dressing. Stacey, go and get a couple of old towels out of your cupboard and tear them into strips. About this wide. Then give 'em to Alexis, OK?" She pointed to one of the women and then ran back into the house.

I fetched two towels from my room, and the big scissors we'd used to cut up the tyre. I could hear Gran talking on the radio. I went back out. Most of the Wonngais except the injured one had got out of the truck now. They'd found the hose we used for filling the dunny bucket and were drinking from it in turn. (From the hose, not the dunny bucket!) Some of them were fooling around, spraying each other.

And suddenly I saw her – Merinda! She must've been behind someone, or maybe hiding.

"Hi, Merinda!" I said. She wasn't fooling around. She looked scared. I know she recognised me, but she didn't make a sign. I went up to her. "Can you help me with these?" She gave that funny little head-twitch, but she held the towel straight while I cut the edge of it and then ripped it into long strips.

She handed them up to the woman called Alexis, who was still in the back of the ute with the hurt man. She looked really worried and I thought she'd been crying, so I guessed he might be her husband. She took the towel strips and started to take the bloodstained cloth off his leg.

"What happened to him? Was there a fight?" I asked Merinda.

She gave her head a shake. She didn't say anything at first, but after a bit she said, "He's my father." And I saw she was nearly crying too. And then I remembered that Gran had said, at the pool that first day, that her mother's name was Alexis. She looked very young to be the mother of someone my age, which Merinda was.

"But what happened?"

"That rubbish Alice mob."

"What'd they do?" She didn't answer. "Is it secret?" She shook her head. "So tell me."

"That fella from Alice Springs, he get full drunk. Roll his car. Finish 'im. My father was there, but he didn't do *nothing*. They give 'im a spearing for that fella who got finish."

"You mean someone speared him on purpose? For a punishment?"

She twitched her head, yes.

Gran came back.

"Bad news, Brando," she said to the driver. "There's been a big bus-smash on the Nullabor, they've had to send two planes, and they can't come out here today, there's no free pilot. You'll have to get him to Laverton yourselves."

"We got no petrol, Auntie."

"Of course you have." He shook his head, looking at the

155

ground. "I told you last time, I'm not giving you any more. We've hardly got enough to get ourselves into town."

"He got to go to hospital," he said quietly.

Gran made some hand signs. He didn't move. She said, "It's not my problem. What if we weren't here? You'll manage somehow."

The men talked among themselves, in a Wonngai language, with lots of hand signs. I edged up to Merinda. She looked really upset. Well, who wouldn't? I put my arm round her.

"He'll be OK," I whispered.

She shook her head. "He got to go to hospital," she said. Her shoulders were shaking.

I didn't know what to say. Merinda's mother had finished changing the dressing, if you could call it that. She handed the bloody cloths to Merinda, who dropped them on the ground. I thought Gran would say something, but she just went into the house, came out with a plastic bag, and picked the dirty cloths up through that. She put them in the empty barrel we burnt rubbish in.

"You got to go along now, Brando. Come on, Stacey. We have to fill the Esky." She turned away and went into the house as if the mob weren't there.

They showed no signs of leaving. I wanted to stay with Merinda but I followed Gran anyway. We went into the kitchen. Gran started packing food. She told me to prepare a bottle for Roo. Every couple of minutes, I looked out of the window and saw they hadn't gone yet.

I wanted to say something, but Gran had a funny stiffness about her that stopped me. We didn't say a word. After another few minutes, Dave came through the back way. "What's going on?" he asked.

"It's the Cosmo mob. Brando and them. Remember that old trouble with the Alice mob about a car accident? Wombley got payback. He's bleeding like a pig. The Flying Doctor can't come. They'll have to deal with it."

I said, "We're going into Laverton anyway. Why can't we take him?"

Gran suddenly lost it.

"And if he died on me? They'd blame *me*. That's how they are, that's payback – someone's always got to be blamed if anyone dies. They're always coming through here with injured people. Not just spear wounds. Boys bleeding from men's business. Women who've been beaten up. And they *always*, *always* say they've run out of petrol! It's not my *fault*. Why should I have to deal with it?"

I'd never seen her like that. Did she hate the Wonngais? I remembered her telling me they'd scared her once. I didn't dare say another word, but Dave came close and put his arm around her.

157

They stood like that with their heads together. He was shorter than her and they looked a bit funny, but suddenly I thought, "He's her boyfriend all right." It's not just the business of, like, sleeping together. She'd worked herself up and shown her not-so-nice side, and he wasn't reproaching her, he was calming her down. Comforting her. Like nobody had comforted my mum, ever, so far as I remembered, I mean, apart from me (once in a while – I was usually too full of myself to bother). I thought, everyone needs that, everyone deserves at least that, someone to put their arms around you when you're upset and behaving badly. Someone to accept you even then. Mum had always done it for me, but when you grow old you haven't got a mum.

Dave said, "We have to take him. You know that."

She pulled out a tissue from her pocket and blew her nose.

"Don't tell me what I know," she said. She stood away from him, back to being herself, and sniffed hard. "Let's get him into the ute."

Chapter Nine

She finished packing what she needed and gave me the Esky to carry to the ute. As I staggered past Merinda with it, I gave her a big smile and a nod. I wished I knew how to hand-signal that it was going to be OK. Not that I could have, with the Esky.

Dave came out. He said a word or two and at once the mob started unloading Wombley off the back of their old wreck. Dave was rearranging stuff in the back of our ute to make room. He spread a swag out for Wombley and put some old cushions and stuff up front near the cabin. He looked at me. "You ready, chook?"

"What about Roo?"

"Where is she?"

That was a thought! Where was she?

"I don't know!" I wailed.

"Go and find her. Fine mother kangaroo you turned out to be."

The first place I looked was where I found her – in her pillowcase. She must have jumped in there and gone to sleep. What a relief! Being a mother must be terrible. Just shocks and frights all the way.

I put her, pillowcase and all, into the back of the ute. Merinda was there, and I said, "Can you look after my baby kangaroo?" She took the bundle in her arms and even smiled a bit when she peeped inside. I fetched Roo's bottle and some big bottles of water. Gran had started the ute up and called to me to hurry. I thought we'd be sitting three in the cabin, but when I got there Dave said, "You're in the back with your baby, mate." Gran said, "Get on with it, Stace!" in her ordering voice and I found myself clambering over the backboard. Merinda, Alexis, Wombley and the young man who'd jumped over the side of the truck were there already. The others had to stay behind. (Come to think of it, I don't know what happened about them. Maybe Gran was right and they had a bit of petrol after all, because they were gone when we got back.)

The ute started to move – I had to scramble along like a crab trying not to step on anyone, finally reached the far end, and sat with my back against the wall of the cabin. I was glad of the cushions for my back, because the metal was practically red hot.

I took the pillowcase with Roo in it on my lap. Merinda was sitting beside me and I gave her one of the cushions. Dave was driving quite slowly because of Wombley, but there was nothing to sit on and I felt as if my backbone would come out of the top of my head every time we went over a bump. It was well hot and dusty, but at least we'd left the flies behind. The Wonngais had brought a whole new lot with them to join ours.

I kept looking at Wombley. He lay with his head beside Alexis's knees. She kept giving him sips of water. He didn't moan or anything, but it must've been hurting like mad because I could see he'd bitten his lips raw and every now and then he kind of writhed. The bumps must have made his pain worse.

The good-looking boy seemed to be along just for the ride. He leant his dusty brown arm along the side of the ute and stared at the scenery.

I nudged Merinda. "Who's he?"

"My brother, Kumina," she said.

I tried to stop thinking about how uncomfortable I was by feeding Roo, and it worked a bit. Merinda watched me kind of hopefully, and after a bit I let her hold Roo and feed her.

When she'd finished she put Roo back in her pillowcase between us on the floor.

"You see *Titanic*?" she asked me out of the blue.

"Yes of course."

"Come on, play Titanic," she said – and stood up! I grabbed her, thinking she'd fall, but she pulled me up beside her. She pulled my hat off and dropped it on the floor. We turned to face the way the ute was going and she showed me how to hold on to the metal rail that was there (only just not too hot to hold). Suddenly we were having fun. The wind blew our hair back and cooled our skin, and I found out how to brace my legs apart and go with the bumps. It was like in *Titanic* when they stand in the front of the ship and she kind of flies. The game was to put your arms out and pretend to fly, and not hold on. Every time we went over a bump I had to grab the rail quick, but Merinda kept her balance.

After a bit we got too much wind and dust in our mouths, so we sat down again and I fell asleep.

When I woke up it was dark and we were in Laverton. The ute was going along quite smoothly now, over a proper road. There were street lights and house lights and shop windows. And people walking and cycling and there were cars and utes and motorbikes. It felt really good being in a town, even a little one like this.

162

The ute pulled up outside a low building like a prefab, with a sign that said "Laverton Hospital". Dave climbed out and said, "All right, chook? Better get out and stretch your legs. Once we get Wombley fixed up in there we'll think about some tucker." Gran was getting out the other side. She and Dave went straight in through the lighted doorway.

Merinda had been asleep, but she woke up now and sat up with a jerk. Alexis was lifting Wombley's head, getting him ready to be moved. Merinda's brother had jumped straight off over the side and gone off into the bushes – for a pee, I expect. I needed one too. Boys are so lucky like that.

A nurse came out with a wheelchair and Dave and Gran helped Alexis to lift Wombley down very carefully. The new bandages were bloody now. It looked like wet, fresh blood. I saw Merinda staring at his leg and I put my arm round her.

"Wait for us on the veranda, girls," said Gran, and they all went in, the nurse pushing the wheelchair.

I looked around for Roo. It was so dark that I couldn't see much, but I could easily pick out the white pillowcase. It lay there on the floor like something just flung away. It was flat. Empty. My heart stopped. I swear, it stopped, right in my chest.

Where was she? What could've happened to her? Could she have jumped overboard? I felt absolutely sick.

Then I saw Kumina. He was standing by the side of the ute. He was just a black shape until he smiled, then I could see his teeth and I could pick out the rest of him.

He had his hands behind his back.

"You lose something?" he asked.

"Yes! My baby kangaroo!"

"Oh, her. I et her up."

I stared at him. "No you didn't," I said, but my mouth was dry. "Where is she?"

He laughed and brought his right hand round. Roo was sitting in the crook of his arm.

"Oh! Roo!"

"Lubly fat one. Make a good cooker," he said.

"Please don't say that! Give her to me!"

He held her in both hands and lifted her to his mouth. "I take one big bite, then I give you," he said, and opened his mouth wide. He looked like some wild man with all his masses of hair and his shining white teeth.

I thought he was really going to do it! I screamed and clutched Merinda. I thought she might say something to him but she didn't. But then he laughed and handed Roo up to me, holding her by the top of her tail. I held her in my arms and cuddled and kissed her. Kumina was still laughing but I felt too upset to care. I knew he'd taken her while we were asleep to play a trick on me and my heart was pounding.

164

I found her bottle. There wasn't much left in it. Kumina was watching me over the side of the ute as I fed her.

"You grow 'im up?"

"Yes. Her mother's dead. It was well mean to scare me like that."

He went on watching. I felt awkward.

"You see a man get the spear?" he asked.

"No, how could I?"

"What about England, they spear 'em there?" he asked.

"No, thank God."

He shrugged and said something in Wonngai to Merinda. Then he rummaged around in the back of the ute, pulled out an old blanket, threw it over his shoulder, and went strolling off down the street.

"What did he say?" I asked, but Merinda wouldn't tell me. "That in England the men aren't strong enough. Was it that?"

She laughed. Then she beckoned me to get off the ute and go on to the hospital veranda. There were people there, patients, mainly Wonngais in hospital clothes, some of them smoking. Merinda seemed to know most of them and they had some talk I couldn't understand. We found a couple of chairs. It felt good to sit down properly. An old Wonngai lady smiled at me and nodded at Roo. I couldn't help suspecting she was thinking how nice she'd taste, especially when she stroked her in an *expert* kind of way, like, feeling how much flesh she had on her.

"Where's Kumina?" I asked.

"Gone for grog. He get thirsty," she said.

"That's a nice name – Kumina."

"He first called for our uncle. But then uncle finish. You can't have a name of—" She stopped.

"Of a dead person?" I guessed.

She gave her little chin-tilt. "Make people sorry. And maybe call that one back. So now he's Kumina – it mean no-name."

I was dying to know about the spearing but I didn't think it was tactful to ask Merinda, so we talked about movies. She'd seen quite a few that I'd seen and we agreed about how good, or bad, most of them were. I began to feel at ease with her. After about half an hour Gran, Dave and Alexis trooped out again, without Wombley.

"They're keeping him in overnight," said Gran. "Lost a packet of blood. You know they pull the spear right through the leg to get it out? The whole length of the shaft. Imagine how it must hurt." I got a picture in my head straight away of pulling the spear through and decided that was all I wanted to know.

Gran, Dave, Alexis, Merinda and me all piled back into the ute (Kumina didn't come back from the pub) and drove out of town along a bumpy old road for about three miles. Once the ute pulled up and Dave got out. I peeped over the side. He was in the headlights, picking up something off the side of the road something squashed. Ugh! What did he want some dead thing for? He put it in a plastic bag.

It was pitch dark now, just starlight, and almost cool. After another ten minutes Dave pulled up and we all got out, dropped the back of the ute and began to drag all the stuff out. I started collecting wood but I didn't get far because Gran called me back. "Come on, Stace, I'll show you how we're going to catch tomorrow's breakfast," she said. She caught my eye in the firelight and I did an eye signal. "You want to come too, Merinda?"

"You gettin' gilgy?"

"Yeah."

She shone her torch on something that looked like a huge paint tin. It had had slits cut into the side of it and a square hole in the lid. Gran was tying a rope to it. "Now we need bait," she said. "Dave, give me that roadkill, will you?"

Dave handed her the plastic bag, and out of it she fished a disgusting squashed rabbit.

"Yuck!" I said. It stank.

"The yabbies don't think so! They love it, the little dears. The condemned will eat a hearty dinner!" She prised off the lid of the tin and dropped the rabbit inside. Then she

167

banged the lid back with a stone. "Come on, girls," she said. "Only mind your step. We don't want the yabbies' dinner to be you."

She led the way along a little stony path, shining the torch back for us. After a bit we came to a sudden stop and she shone her torch down over the edge of something like a cliff. Far down below there was black water, a sort of lake, just glinting a little in the starlight. I sucked in my breath. If we'd have kept on walking...! Gran was lowering the tin with the rabbit in it down the cliff, into the water. I shone the torch and watched it sink out of sight. Then Gran tied the end of the rope to something sticking out of the ground.

"What are yabbies?"

"You'll see in the morning. The trap'll be full of 'em."

I didn't want to show my ignorance in front of Merinda. I just hoped it wasn't something gross like eels.

We saw the fire when we were still a way from the campsite. It looked very friendly and nice, glowing away, showing us where to head for. When we got nearer I saw that it was two fires, about twenty metres apart. "Why two fires?" I asked Gran. She gave me a quick look.

"One for us, one for them," she said.

"Oh, aren't they camping with us?"

"They like their own fire and their own patch. But they like to be near us. There's safety in numbers."

"Safety?"

"Listen, Stacey, there's nothing to be scared of."

I hadn't been, till then. "What do you mean?"

"I don't want you to get nervous. And don't you start telling your scary stories, Merinda. We all have things we're scared of, but most of 'em aren't real, they're just notions, like ghosts."

Merinda ran off to join her mother.

It felt really good to get back to the firelit circle, and Dave. Good old Dave. You need a man sometimes. For protection.

Dave had fixed up the beds. He'd rolled his swag out on the bare ground, and set up Gran's old iron shearer's bed with her swag on it. He'd spread mine in the back of the ute, like before.

Gran was mixing some flour and water into a dough. I asked what she was making. "Damper," she said. "It's a kind of bread, like the old miners used to eat."

"Will it take long?" I asked, looking over at Merinda and Alexis, sitting by their fire.

"Why, d'you want to go visiting?"

"Can I?"

"Sure! Why not? Only don't eat any of their Wonngai pie, you've got your own grub."

I thought Wonngai pie must be some real bush food like I'd heard about, but I found they'd taken the top off a Fray

Bentos tinned chicken pie and stood it on the hot ashes by the fire. I love those meat pies at home, but I couldn't imagine one without the pastry top crisped in a proper oven. I asked Merinda what they'd do for sleeping, without swags.

"Doona," she said. She showed me two quilt-things they were sitting on, very old and tatty.

"Aren't you scared of snakes and spiders and scorpions?" She laughed and shook her head.

It took a while for the pie to cook so we sat cross-legged around their fire and nobody talked, but I thought of the bikies at Christmas so I said, "Let's each tell a story."

Then I felt embarrassed in case it was the wrong thing to say, but Merinda turned to me right away and said, "You first." So I had to think of something.

I couldn't. But then Merinda said, "Tell about – you know," and she pointed to my stomach. I told about how Mum and me had had a row, and made it up by getting our bellybuttons pierced together. That went down well. Merinda made me show my bellybutton ring to Alexis. They both felt it in the dark, and Merinda asked her something in Wonngai and I could *almost* understand. I certainly understood Alexis's answer, because she clapped both hands over her belly and shook her head and laughed and almost rolled over backwards, so I knew Merinda had asked her if she'd agree to have her bellybutton pierced mother-and-daughter style with her.

So then it was Merinda's turn. She hid her face at first, but I said, "Go on, I told mine." So in the end she told this really weird story.

"One time I make my cousin cry by teasin' her properly. So she get *re-eally* mad and she push me down flat and she laid on toppa me and she put her goanna in me. And he go in my doony from her doony and bite me and scratch me and I scream for the pain and then her uncle come and make her take it back."

That was it. I waited for more but there wasn't any. Finally I said, "What do you mean, she put her goanna in you? What goanna?"

Merinda looked at Alexis. Alexis said, "Goanna her mubrun animal, live in her doony." She touched her stomach.

"Let me get this right. This girl had a big lizard living in her stomach?"

They both nodded. I was sure they were having me on, but they weren't smiling. I said, "But she couldn't have. It would eat *her*."

"No. Cos it her mubrun."

"What's a mubrun?"

"Totem," said Alexis.

"But how could it get into *your* – er – doony?"

"She laid on me, doony to doony, and she send it."

A goose walked over my grave. (Or maybe it was a goanna!) Of course I didn't believe one word of it, but the weird thing was, Merinda did, and so did Alexis. Merinda had really felt a goanna inside her. It was impossible to me, but not to her. I couldn't even turn it away by laughing.

We were quiet and sat watching the Wonngai pie beginning to bubble. I'd brought Roo with me, and now she stood next to me, scratching her back the way she did with one front paw like a little old man, and I put my arm around her and played with her long ears.

Dave called me. "Come on, chook, grub's nearly ready."

"I'm coming," I called back, but I didn't move. There was this funny atmosphere around the Wonngai fire. Somehow only the Fray Bentos was part of my world. Everything else was strange. Weird. Then, just as I was going to get up and go back to my own fire, Alexis started to tell her story and I couldn't leave.

She started by smoothing out the ground between her and the fire with her hand, to make a flat place in the dust like a fan. Then she drew a wavery line with her finger, from the top near the fire, to near her feet.

"One night this woman been campin' out bush by a creek. Her and her husband and one little girl." She made three dots in the dust beside the creek-line. "That woman, she was a dumb half-caste woman. She didn't know Wonngai law. She didn't know it was a mamu creek."

I wanted to ask what mamu meant, but I was afraid she'd stop.

"The man just come back from bush with a kangaroo, lubly fat one. They made a fire and cook 'im and had a feed. Then they layin' down to sleep. But they hear a whistle from a big gumtree." All the time she was making little dots to show what was happening, that I could just see by firelight. She didn't draw a tree, but she made a special mark for it.

"They didn't know there was a mamu up there. That mamu looked like a little-girl-woman, little girl with a white hair and red eyes.

"That lady she put her little kid to sleep between 'em and then her and the man went to sleep. But that dumb woman didn't know you meant to cover the kid with a doona."

I was getting mixed up with doonas and doonys. But I didn't want to interrupt.

"You not allowed to give them a fresh air. You gotta cover their faces with a doona. That kid was layin' there awake and when that lady was asleep, that mamu girl-woman come down from the tree and grabbed the kid and that mamu swapped that kid with a mamu kid. And she took the lady's good kid away. So the lady had a mamu kid now instead of her kid."

Dave called me again. "Come on, Stace, can't you smell the damper?" But I hardly heard him.

"That mamu kid started screamin' properly and that lady, she been waked up and she been looked at that kid that been layin' between 'em and start screamin' too. It had a teeth like a daggers and hair white like old woman and spiky. The lady threw the mamu kid away and been screamin', 'Where my kid, where my kid?' And then her man wake up."

Dave was coming across to get me. He stopped just short of the firelight circle and listened. Alexis was sweeping her hand across the dirt, wiping away the dots and marks that made the story. Now she drew the creek in again and put the people in in new places. After that, her fingers just told the story along with her words.

"The woman cryin' and askin' him to bring their kid back. So he got up and he looked on the ground and he saw tracks and he started chasin' after, and that tracks led him all the way over the hill to this one big huge gumtree. And the man, he been get that big yubbu rock and chuck it at that mamu little-girl-woman. And that mamu dropped the kid she steal, down from the tree."

"Stacey, you should come now!" said Dave.

"Shhh!" I said, really sharply. I *needed* to know how it would end.

"The father been run and catch it and the mamu came down from the tree and tried to grab the kid off the man again, but that man got another yubbu and throwed it at the mamu head. The mamu been ran away and the father took his little girl back to the mother and they packed up and left. They gone back to town."

"Good thinking," grunted Dave. He bent down and hiked me to my feet. "Say goodnight, Stacey," he said as if I was five years old. But I got it. He was worried about me listening to all this scary stuff.

"Thanks, Alexis, that was a really great story," I said over my shoulder as Dave led me away, holding my elbow. I'd picked Roo up by the tail, like Kumina had – she just hung there, she didn't mind. "Goodnight!" I yelled back as we reached our fire. But I could see they'd turned their backs and probably started on the Wonngai pie.

I sat down beside our fire and took a big hot chunk of bread from Gran. She'd baked it in foil in the embers and it tasted good. She had a tin of meat to go with it but it didn't smell as good as the Wonngai pie.

Dave was telling Gran in a quiet voice about the mamu story.

"Did it scare you, Stacey?" she asked.

"No!" I said. "Of course not." But to tell the truth, it had, a bit. "What is a mamu, anyway?"

175

"What do you think it is?"

"A – a sort of bogeyman?"

"Or woman. Yeah. Near enough. A bad spirit, but worse than that. Because it's solid."

I wanted to say, "But it's not real, is it?" just to hear her say it wasn't, because she was talking as if it was. But I thought that was silly. *Of course* it wasn't real.

When Roo and I were snuggled into my swag, she fell asleep right away. It was lovely having her in my swag with me, although every now and then she was restless and kicked me. She had these really strong back legs. But I couldn't sleep, not for a long time. I had all kinds of thoughts, the nicest ones I could, but then I couldn't keep it away any more. I started thinking about the mamu.

That was one spooky story. And I couldn't just dismiss it, because... well, because of the way everyone behaved in it. The way the mother left the little girl to sleep without covering her face to hide her from the mamu. She was too ignorant. And it was stolen by this horrible creature that I could see in my imagination. Not a bogeyman. A witch. A horrible, ugly, grotesque witch.

Strange as it was, I'd heard something like it before. Fairies, or goblins or whatever, stealing children and leaving goblin-children behind. They were called changelings. We did *A Midsummer Night's Dream* at school and there was one in that.

But in the mamu story, the father got the little girl back. He fought the mamu and caught the kid before it hit the ground. I liked that part. I liked the father being brave and going after the mamu. The mother might've been stupid and not known how to protect her, but the father rescued her.

I snuggled Roo in my arms and tried to shake off the mamu feeling. But then I started thinking of Merinda and another girl lying face to face on the ground and some magic happening that made Merinda think a goanna was eating her. How could she believe that? How could anyone?

My teacher once tried to tell us that people are basically the same all over the world. It was to make us tolerant. But I knew now that me and Merinda were just about as different as we could be. It wasn't about her being black and me white. Of course not. Only one out of every ten kids at my school is white, but it's like we're all about the same. But me and Merinda, we lived differently and we believed different things, and were scared of different things, and that made us different even if we liked the same movies, because that's surface, and this other business was deep.

I tried to imagine Loretta getting mad at me and… but it was no good. Imagining myself back in London, back at school, and then thinking about magic and totems just didn't make sense. It only made a sort of bush-sense. It was weird. Like another world with other-world people.

Merinda must have a totem animal. I wondered what. Then I started wondering what mine would be if I had one. I rolled over on my back and stared at the stars. I scanned the whole wide sky.

And there, right on the horizon, was a bunch of stars that looked sort of like my (nearly pet) scorpion, only vast. I could see his tail, curving up into the night sky.

OK. That would be my mubrun – my totem. I could borrow an Australian one. Somehow giving myself a totem made me feel I'd made a sort of bridge between me and this place. After that it was easy to fall asleep. It was as if I'd had the right thoughts, and been allowed to.

In the dead of night, though, I woke up. Something had woken me.

I leant up on my elbow and looked over the side of the ute. There was no moon, it was black-dark, just the stars and the remains of the fires. I saw them both glowing dimly, little round red patches in the blackness. Then I heard it again – a sharp whistling noise…

Gran had said you should never camp or park under a tree, so the nearest was far off. But that's where the whistling seemed to be coming from. In a flash I remembered the mark Alexis had made on the ground for a tree, and I remembered the one for a mamu, the white-haired red-eyed girl-woman, crouching on a branch holding the little stolen girl… Then I heard another whistle, this time from where Merinda and Alexis were.

My breathing stopped. Suddenly some terrifying *something* was right beside the ute. I could see it, looming up, blocking the red fire-patches.

I screamed. And then a hand came and covered my mouth. I panicked and started to struggle.

"Shut up, chook, it's only me!"

It was Dave. He let me go. I was panting and trembling.

"You scared the crap out of me!" I shouted, and started to cry. I could see a bit more now. I could see Gran sitting up on her iron bed. "What's going on?" she called.

"I thought she might be scared of the whistling," said Dave. He sounded a bit scared himself, which wasn't like him. "I was just seeing she was OK."

I tried to calm down. My heart was whacking inside my ribs. I'd frightened poor little Roo, too, she was trying to struggle out of the sleeping bag. "I don't care about the stupid whistling," I muttered, looking for something to blow my nose on. "Who's doing it, anyhow?"

"It's just some visitors for Alexis," said Dave. "That whistling's what they do, to find each other at night. I bet our mob will be off to join the other mob, they're probably camped out by the pit somewhere."

"I – I thought it was the mamu," I admitted. I'd found a tissue in my pocket.

Dave turned his head as if he thought someone might be listening.

"Don't talk like that," he said very quietly. "There's no mamus."

I wished he'd sounded surer, or at least talked in a normal voice. I didn't sleep much for the rest of the night.

In the morning Gran shook me to wake me up. "Time for the yabby trap!" she said. I struggled awake and she helped me down. Dave was boiling water in a blackened old billy on the fire. I looked towards where Merinda and Alexis had been but there was nothing but a black circle from their dead fire. I ran over to see if there was anything left of the picture-story. But it was all rubbed out.

I wished Merinda hadn't gone. But daylight made everything seem normal and unscary.

Gran strode along through the scrub with me behind her till we got to the edge of this pit. By day I could see it was big, a huge hole in the ground with steep sloping sides and water in it, and just a little beach of stones in one place where you could get near the water.

Gran said, "That's not a real natural lake, you know. It's an old open-cut gold mine that got worked out, so the town diverted a creek to fill it with water and now you can swim in it."

She looked all around. There was nobody. "Would you like a swim?" she asked. "We could go in in the nick."

"You mean, skinny? What about Dave?"

"He came down earlier. It was him suggested it. Don't worry, he'll stay away."

So we walked down to the low place and stripped off and went into the lake. It was absolute heaven, much nicer than the swimming pool somehow, just the two of us breaking the dead flat water of this great lake, like cutting a sheet of grey silk, with the sun creeping over the tall side of it and flooding our pit-world with gold. "It's like all the gold that was taken out of the ground here is coming back to its place," I said. Gran looked at me across the water.

"That's nice," she said. "You've got a good imagination, Stace."

I stretched out and swam. I felt like some water nymph or something, or a jungle girl. I got lovely and clean and cool. I didn't think many Grans would do this. I didn't know what surprises mine still had for me.

We dried ourselves off with some of our clothes and then climbed up to the top again, found the rope and I helped Gran haul the trap back up. It came up slowly, dragging against the side of the pit and streaming water out of its slits. Along with the water noise I could hear a rattling sound.

"Hear that? They're tap-dancing."

I couldn't wait to see the yabbies. Gran was grinning as she prised the lid off with a piece of metal and peered inside. "Good catch! Have a look."

I peeped in. There wasn't much of the rabbit left. In the bottom were dozens of little grey things moving about. Gran reached in and lifted one out. It was like a tiny grey lobster, waving its little claws.

"Ugh! What are they?"

"They're freshwater crayfish. Delicious! Come on, I'm starving!"

She almost ran back, holding the wet tin by a handle of rope. When we got there, she took the lid off the billy, which was boiling, and she murdered those yabbies by dropping them, a few at a time, into the water. Cruel or what? Gran and Dave were chatting away happily and getting plates and pannikins out (there was another billy for coffee). When the yabbies had turned pink, Gran fished them out with a slotted spoon on to three plates.

"I don't want any," I said. I did in a way, I love prawns and these were just about like prawns, but I felt upset and a bit sick, seeing them die like that. I half expected Gran to try to talk me into eating them but she didn't.

"All the more for us," she said, and divided my portion between her and Dave. She got out a jar of mayonnaise and some leftover damper and they ate the lot, throwing the shells and heads in the fire. I had an apple. Even that I only ate half of, and threw the rest away. Gran went straight off and fetched it back.

"Waste not, want not," she said, just like Nan would. "If you don't want it, try feeding it to Roo. Little bits."

I tried. Gran showed me how to take bites and chew them and then pass them down my front to her. She began by sniffing them and after a while, she did eat them a little. It felt sort of sweet, the way she nibbled my fingers.

"You see? You're weaning her," said Gran, "just like a real baby. Here, try her on some rolled oats," and she gave me some porridge oats out of a bag. Roo seemed even keener on those and after that, as I didn't have any more milk, I filled her bottle with water and she drank that. I felt like a successful mother kanga and I forgot about the yabbies.

After we'd packed up, we drove back into Laverton.

Gran dropped me off in the middle of town. She and Dave had to collect some fuel and do shopping for stores, so I got to wander about the town by myself. It was funny – the Wonngais didn't look so strange to me any more. I was taking them for granted. After a bit I thought I'd go and visit Wombley in the hospital.

I found it easily, it's such a little town. I went to the desk and said, "Can I see Wombley?"

"Who?"

"His name's Wombley. He came in last night. He'd been speared."

"Oh, him," she said. "Are you a relative?"

Did I look like one? I couldn't resist, so I said, "Yes, he's my uncle," with a dead straight face. Ask a silly question!

"Well, does he expect you?"

"No."

She leant towards me. "Aborigines are shy, you know. He may not be pleased to see you if he doesn't know you well."

I didn't know what to say to that, so I just stood there. After a minute she said, "Oh well, why not? Since his family haven't shown up." She came out from behind the desk and led me through a few corridors – it wasn't a very big place, not like a proper hospital, but it felt kind of friendly and homely – and into a room where there were three beds. Only one of them was occupied, and there was Wombley, sitting up with a tray-thing in front of him, eating his lunch.

He looked up at me and his face sort of froze with surprise. I hoped it was surprise, and not, like, not wanting me to be there.

"Hi," I said. "Remember me? I'm Stacey."

He swallowed and his head sort of shivered. It wasn't a real nod, and after one quick look at me he turned his face away.

"I thought I'd come and visit you," I said.

He stopped eating. There was a long uncomfortable silence. What could I talk about? Food, that was safe. "What's the grub like here?" I asked. "The tucker, I mean."

He showed me his plate. It was some white meat, potatoes and peas and a side salad.

"Is it good?"

"Yeah. Not bad."

"We had yabbies for breakfast where we camped. Near the pit. The old gold mine." I paused between sentences to give him a chance to say something, but he didn't. "Actually I didn't eat the yabbies, er – gilgies. They looked good, though."

"You don't like gilgy?"

"I've never had them. I like other shellfish. I didn't like seeing them put in the boiling water."

Suddenly a big grin came on his face. "Yeah?" he said. "Kids like that part."

"You don't mind killing things?"

He shook his head. "Hunting's good," he said. "You got a gun?"

"My grand— My *gubalee* has one. She keeps it in the ute."

185

"Yeah. Auntie's a good shot. I went out shooting with her one time. She shot a marlu right between the teeth."

"What's a marlu?"

"Red kangaroo. You shoot kangaroo?"

"I've never shot anything."

"You learn to shoot kangaroo," he said. "Good bush tucker." He kept glancing at the bulge in my shirt.

"Maybe," I said. "Only not this one." I fished Roo out and put her on the bed beside Wombley.

He petted her a bit, and I watched as he fed her some bits of lettuce. She ate it quite eagerly now.

"I suppose you'd like to eat *her*," I said.

"When she get big. Not now. Feed her good tucker, make her big and fat, then eat her." I couldn't tell if he was teasing me or if he meant it.

I scooped Roo up and put her back in my top. "Do you think Merinda and Alexis and… your son will come and visit you?"

"I'll go along tomorrow, must be."

Healed up by tomorrow! I thought. *You'll be lucky.*

"Please tell them I said hello," I said. "I hope you get better soon. I have to go now."

Wombley'd gone back to his dinner. I went to the door, and then, I couldn't help it, I turned round and asked my question.

186

"Did you let them spear you – the Alice mob? I mean – you agreed to it?"

"Yeah," he said.

"Why?"

"Payback."

"But Merinda said you didn't do anything. So what did they pay you back for?"

He looked up at me sharply, his fingers still in his mouth. Then he looked away. I thought he wasn't going to answer me. Then he said, "I been in whitefella jail once. Bad place. I don't go 'nother time."

I didn't really understand. Had he let them spear him *instead* of going to jail? It wasn't a real answer. But he wasn't going to say any more. I turned to leave. But then he said, "You see your daddy?"

I turned back quickly. "Do you know my father?"

"I know 'im," he said, busy with his lunch.

"How? When?"

"When we was little fellas."

"Were you friends?"

"Yeah. Me and Blue. Proper mates." Blue. Dad had blue eyes like mine. But I'd never heard him called that. It was something from his other life, when he grew up on the station.

"I haven't seen him for ages," I said. He stopped eating. "Two years at least."

187

He became really still, bent over his tray, his food halfway to his mouth. He held it like that for about a minute. Then he went on eating as if I wasn't there. I had the strangest feeling I was missing something. I didn't want to leave till I found out what. But I had to, because he was, like, dismissing me.

I went out of the room and out of the hospital and went to look for Gran and Dave.

Chapter Ten

On the way back to the station we rode three in the front. It was crowded but more comfortable than the back.

"What did you do with yourself in town?" Gran asked.

"I went to visit Wombley."

They both turned to look at me. Then they looked across me at each other, like they didn't quite believe I'd said it.

"You did, eh? And how did he react when you marched into his room?"

"He was nice. He was eating his lunch. We talked."

"What about?"

"He said – he said he knew my dad. When they were kids. He called him Blue."

"That's right, come to think of it. That mob used to

come around a lot. Wombley and Darren used to play footie together in the yard."

"He just asked me if I'd seen him. Only he…"

"What?"

"It was like he was trying to say something else." I frowned while I thought just what Wombley'd said. "You see your daddy?" See. Like he was there in front of us. Like Wombley could see him and I couldn't.

And all at once I could see him, my dad I mean, in my mind. Really clear.

Nothing special about that, you might think. But it was two years since I'd really seen him, and just recently I hadn't been able to imagine him. Now all of a sudden, I could. I saw his tall body and his blond hair and his smile. I've done nothing but slag him off, writing this, calling him useless and a loser. But imagining him playing football with Wombley when they were both little fellas made me realise something.

Dad's trouble was, he sort of never grew up, he went on being like a kid himself, and when I was a kid, that was good for me. He was never too busy to play with me and he liked to play kids' games as much as I did. He was crazy about "footie" and taught me to kick a ball around in the park. He bought me a train set, and when I didn't like it much, he played with it himself, but he found a way to bring my toy animals into his train-games. He took me to movies and we chewed gum and ate chips and pizzas in the street and licked ice lollies together, and he talked to me just like another kid would, and teased and told jokes and sang songs and played silly tricks.

Later that really got on my nerves cos it seemed so childish, but at the time it made me love him like mad. I'd never let Mum say a word against him, and when she nagged him, about getting work for example, I always stood up for him. Until I was about eleven. Then I went over to her side because I saw that she was the one keeping the family together, earning the money and that, and that a lot of his silliness came from drinking.

And then, right after my twelfth birthday, he left us. After that I never remembered one good thing about him. Till now.

Gran was still talking.

"Once I remember Wombley took him off bush and they didn't come back for twenty-four hours – I was sick with worry. It was when his mother and some other women were hunting honey ants. I knew his mum quite well. She died of diabetes when she was only thirty-three. Wombley came to tell me."

We drove on for a while, and then I said, "How do you hunt honey ants?" I remembered Merinda and her pal had said something about me eating them when I was too young. It must be the local joke if you're different.

"The women do it. They tap the ground till they hear it's hollow. Then they sit and dig with crowbars till they've dug a big hole. Then they pick out the honey ants. They're about so big –" she held her fingers about two centimetres apart "– and their abdomen is like a bubble. You put their back ends in your mouth and suck, and in goes the honey. Yum, yum."

I shuddered, thinking of the poor ants going pop. Worse than the yabbies, really. "Have you had some?"

"Oh, sure. I used to go out hunting with the Wonngais a lot when I was here by myself, before Dave came."

"I thought you said you were scared of them."

"Only when they're drunk. Grog is really bad for them. They know it and a lot of 'em keep off it, but some of them can't stop."

We drove on in silence for a while. I was thinking.

"Wombley said he'd been to jail."

"Did you know he'd been locked up, Dave?" asked Gran, leaning across me.

"Yeah, I heard something." After a bit, Dave added, "It's worse for them. I heard he nearly went crazy inside. They caught him trying to hang himself."

* * *

192

We didn't do anything special at New Year. Well, no, that's not true either, something special did happen, I just didn't know it was at the time.

Gran made a nice meal – I'd actually asked her to buy some salad and she made a big one with avocados and croutons. Dave wouldn't touch it, he said he wasn't a rabbit and where was the *meal*, meaning meat, and he got quite bad-tempered and drank a lot of beer from the new supply. He fell asleep while we were washing up.

And afterwards Gran gave me a New Year present. She hadn't wrapped it or anything. It was a big yellow writing pad with lines, and some biros. It was that night I started writing down some of the stuff that'd happened. Not like I'm writing it now, from afterwards. Just bits, like the stories Merinda and Alexis had told, and about Roo, and Humpy White. And Kumina (I described Kumina in detail – I think I must have fancied him a bit) and Wombley. What turned out special was that I was never bored in the evenings after that. There weren't enough hours after dark to write all I wanted to. I thought Dave would get grumpy because I asked him not to turn the generator off until later and later. But he didn't.

But anyway it was getting near the time for me to go home.

School was due to start on the eighth of January, and as soon as New Year passed I started getting myself ready to leave.

Packing wouldn't take long, but getting ready meant getting my head around leaving everything here. Especially Roo.

I spent a long time with her every day, talking to her and that. Of course, kangaroos don't understand much, but she flicked her ears and looked at me with her little button eyes and I kidded myself that she understood. Gran'd said back at the beginning that we could give her to a wildlife park and she'd be happy there with other kangas and never have to worry about some Kumina coming along and hunting her.

"When are we going to the wildlife park, Gran?" I asked right after New Year.

Gran looked vague. "Oh, soon," she said, and went off in the ute to check a windmill.

That left me alone with Dave, and Dave was in a funny mood. He wasn't being so friendly with me any more. He never teased me and he didn't even call me chook. He seemed sort of sullen, he kept to himself and did his work around the place, and, it seemed to me, as often as he could he drove off in the Toyota to check on the cattle or something that kept him away from the house. I had a strong idea that this was somehow to do with me, but I honestly couldn't think why.

So I asked him.

"What's wrong, Dave?" I said.

"Nothing, what d'you mean?"

"Have I done something?"

"Course not," he said, kind of gruff.

"So why are you acting funny?"

"Don't be stupid," he said, and walked away from me.

That night when Gran came home, I said, "Is the wildlife park on the way back to Perth?"

"Why?"

Why? Wasn't it obvious? "So we can drop Roo off on our way to the airport, and not make a separate journey. I want to keep her as long as I can."

Gran gave me a funny look out the sides of her eyes. Like she was hiding something. A sort of shiver went down my back. I didn't know why at the time. I just sensed something not right.

"You don't want to part from her, do you?"

"No, of course not. But I'll have to."

"Wouldn't you like to keep her for ever?"

I thought that was just a silly thing to say. I said, "How could I keep her for ever? I can't take her home with me."

"Well. We'll see when the time comes," she said. Which was a ridiculous answer when you think of it. Either the park *was* on the way to Perth or it wasn't.

Now I did start counting days.

When we'd been in Laverton I'd asked Gran if I could phone Nan on a public phone. She'd said yes but then after they'd been shopping she said the phone was broken and there was no time. But still she found time for me to buy a postcard and send it to Nan, though I knew I'd be home before it could get there, probably.

Every time I tried to talk to Gran about leaving, she put me off. Not that I could catch her much. Suddenly she seemed to be incredibly busy – always off somewhere. Windmills, she said. And without taking me. She was just never *around*.

Now I had only four days left. Four days to drive to Perth, fly back to London and get ready for school. It didn't seem nearly enough. I began to panic.

It was Dave I talked to. Who else was there?

"Dave, has Gran told you when we're leaving?"

"No," he said, and tried to walk away from me, but I wasn't having any and I got in front of him.

"But I have to get home! School starts in four days."

He stopped. He looked at the ground. He couldn't meet my eyes. And all at once I felt like something clutched at my heart. It was fear. Because suddenly I knew. It couldn't be true – but it was.

"She's not going to send me back," I said slowly, like I was talking through a fog of shock. "Is she?"

"Ask her."

"She won't say anything! She won't even tell me when my return flight is!"

And then he blew.

"I'll tell you when it is. It's the day after tomorrow! I've had it out with her – not once, either!" he shouted, so that I jumped away. "Crazy woman! She brings you here – you come all this way with her – and what? She's *stolen* you! Yeah! You didn't know that, did you? That you've been kidnapped?" We stared at each other. His eyes were all red as if he was going to cry. He grabbed me quickly and gave me a hug.

"I'd take you to Perth myself and put you on the plane, but she's hidden your passport and nothing I can say will make her cough it up. She's quite a woman, but sometimes she gets a bee in her bonnet and she's just plain nuts!"

He let me go, and rubbed his hands all over his face, the way he did when he was in a state. I burst into tears.

"But why, Dave? Why would she do that?"

"Oh, she's got her reasons. She'd reason the possums out of the trees. 'What's she going back to? An empty rotten little flat in that filthy rainy city, nobody to look after her, a runaway dad and a mother who thinks *he's* her first priority! She's better off here where we can take care of her.'" He stopped and his mouth kind of worked as if he was chewing something sour. "She's right in a way, but I told her, you can't do that without asking her, she's not a baby!"

"Was – was that her idea right from the beginning? When she first brought me?"

"Fair go, I think she meant to send you back, but… Well. When you were visiting Wombley and we were getting the stores, she went off and made a phone call to your place."

"She said the phone was bust!" I yelled.

"She lied. There was no answer. Of course, I told her – your mum might've been out, but oh no, Glendine decides she's off somewhere with your dad and that's it, she flat out refuses to send you back. Looks like you're stuck here, chook. I'm sorry."

Chapter Eleven

First we searched the house, Dave and me. I reckoned he should know all the possible places where she could've hidden my passport, but we couldn't find it. I felt more and more frantic and he got quieter and quieter. In the end we gave up. He slammed a drawer shut so hard the wall shook, and stamped into the kitchen without a word.

I was in a cold rage. I was going to give it to her, the minute she got back. Curry? Even Madras ones don't come any hotter than what I had ready for her.

Normally, when she'd go out without me, I'd get a bit of food ready. I knew she liked that. But not now. I fed the chooks of course, no reason for them to go hungry, but nothing more. It was the fourth of January and I meant to leave early the next morning, come hell or high water, as

Grandad used to say.

I sat on the veranda with Roo beside me, just seething.

I heard Dave at the fridge and knew he was going for the beer. I even heard the cans popping open one by one. I found I was counting them. It was a lot of beer, even in Australia. He stumbled out to the dunny, then went back in without speaking and I heard two more pops. I was hot and uncomfortable but I refused to go indoors. I was going to be there, waiting for her. I went over and over what I had to say to her.

"How could you steal me? How could you think I'd want to stay here for ever with someone who'd do that? I trusted you! You're nothing better than a kidnapper!" I got myself worked up so much I was crying.

She didn't come.

It was dead hot. The flies were driving me crazy. One landed on my mouth and I was so mad I slapped myself quite hard, trying to kill it. That sort of brought me to my senses. I stopped crying and decided to go indoors and pack. I was going to be absolutely ready. So I did that, all except my sponge bag and my travel clothes, and I put my suitcase out on the veranda so she'd see it sitting there and know I meant business.

Dave was asleep on the sofa. His latest can of beer was half hanging from his hand, and the dregs were dripping on the floor. I took it away from him and stood looking at him for a moment. Good old Dave. No wonder he'd been acting strange. He was worried about me, worried about what Gran was doing. I nearly bent down and kissed him, but he was too sweaty.

Then I went out and sat in the shade house for a bit. I kept listening for the ute. But she still didn't come, and it was so hot I lay down on the shearer's bed and fell asleep.

The sound of voices woke me up.

I came-to kind of slowly. When I first jumped up I had to sit down again. After a minute I got my act together and went outside. But it wasn't Gran. It was Kumina and Wombley.

Wombley was on his feet, but with a stick to help him walk. I looked around for their truck but there wasn't one. They'd come on foot. How far? How could Wombley have got better so quickly with two great holes in his thigh? Maybe Wonngais know how to heal themselves with magic plants or something.

"Hello," I said.

"Where's your gubalee?"

"She's not here."

"Dave here?"

"He's asleep."

"You wake 'im up," said Wombley.

"Why, what for? Where's your truck?"

"Battery trouble. You get Dave."

I went into the house. Dave was still lying there. He was snoring now. I gave him a shake and when that didn't work, I called him, and then shouted in his ear. He didn't even grunt. He was right out of it – slaughtered.

I went back out.

"I can't wake him," I said.

"He been on the grog?"

"Yeah. Properly." I liked using that word like them.

"Dave not full drunk, not 'im."

"Well, he is."

There was a long silence. They stared around at anything but me.

"You drive that one, Stacey?" asked Wombley at last, pointing to the Toyota with his chin. The Toyota was the ute Dave usually drove. It was newer than Gran's.

"Me? No. Only the old ute." I waited. "Why? Do you want a lift back to your truck?"

"Not our truck. 'Nother truck. He roll 'im. Then he gone walkabout."

"Who did, the driver?"

Kumina started to say something, but Wombley stopped him. "Yeah," said Wombley. "That driver, he go bush. We gotta find 'im."

"But he'll come back to the truck. Won't he?"

"Maybe not. Them tracks he make tell he painin' plenty, maybe nearly finished. If we don't find 'im maybe he finish properly."

"Well, I can't do anything."

"Yeah, you can. You can easy drive that one. Follow 'em tracks. We show you."

I didn't know what to do. They stood there, waiting. I finally said, "Can't you drive, Wombley?"

"No. We don't drive Dave's car. And my leg's painin'. You gotta drive."

"Where's your truck?"

"That way. Close up. Our truck finish. No battery. Kumina stall 'im when we stop. No one to push."

I went back in the house and had another go at waking Dave, but I thought, even if I do wake him, he won't be fit to drive. What could I do? I *could* do nothing at all, that's what I *could* do. Why should I risk trying to drive the Toyota that I'd never driven? I was scared. But something in me, some prideful thing, made me think, *If I can drive the old ute I can drive the Toyota.* Dave told me it was a doddle to drive cos it had power steering. Easier than the heavy old ute. Only it was much newer and he knew Gran wouldn't let me drive it.

I knew where the keys were. I took them. I remembered

that Gran had said you should never go driving without a bottle of water, so I fetched one from the fridge. I left Roo sleeping in her pillowcase and went out to the others. (I didn't even give her a kiss. *I didn't even give her a kiss!*)

"OK," I said, taking a deep breath. "Show me where."

The first part was dead easy. Dave was right about the Toyota being easier to drive.

Kumina sat in the open back and Wombley sat in the passenger seat next to me. When we got to the main road, Wombley pointed left, towards Laverton. I found myself getting excited and driving a bit too fast. It was even fun, in a scary kind of way. But Wombley flapped his hand to tell me to slow down.

After about a mile I saw the Wonngais' truck. It was just stuck in the middle of the road. On the other side was another one. I could just see it. It had run off the road and up this high ridge of earth there, and rolled over the other side. Now it lay with its wheels and its underneath facing us. There was nobody near it. I pulled across the road and stopped and the Wonngais got out, Kumina doing his cat-jump and Wombley getting out slowly with one leg stiff.

Kumina beckoned me to get out too, and pointed to the road. "One marlu got in front of him and he swerve. You not meant to swerve for a roo, you meant to hit him. You swerve, you can roll, like 'im."

"How do you know a roo jumped out?"

"Tracks on the road." He showed me. "Look here, see. Marlu come out of this way. Truck comin', roo went that way. Truck went that way – bang."

He led the way over the ridge and round to the other side of the truck. I looked in through the windscreen. There were some beer cans lying on the inside of the door, where it lay on the ground. Maybe the driver was drunk.

Kumina crouched down and showed me a sort of scuffled bit of earth, and then, when he pointed close, I could make out footprints going off into the bush.

I looked in that direction. It was pretty open. There were just a few trees dotted about, small mulgas and a few bigger gumtrees. You'd see someone if he was anywhere nearby.

"Where's he gone?" I asked.

"That way, must be." Kumina pointed away from the road.

And he set off at a trot, looking at the ground.

Wombley called me from the far side of the earth bank. I climbed to the top. Wombley said, "He track 'im. We go in the one-tonner."

"*What?* You mean, drive off the road?"

"Yeah. Follow 'im." He nodded at Kumina who was already about twenty metres away.

"I can't drive in the bush!" I said. "I'm not a good enough driver! Besides, Gran said it's dangerous to leave the road, you can get lost."

"Nobody get lost," said Wombley, grinning.

Now I was really scared. Standing up high on the ridge, I looked around. The ground was all bumpy. There were tall, spiky tufts of that spinifex grass everywhere. There were dead branches. Gran'd told me about times when she'd run on a "stake" as she called it, and punctured her tyre. What would I do if I got a puncture?

"Come down, Stacey."

I ran down. Wombley sort of steered me back to the Toyota.

"Wombley, I'm not—"

"You put 'im in four-wheel drive first. See that narba on the hub?" He pointed to a silver thing like a tiny tin can sticking out of the middle of the wheel. "You turn 'im that way." He showed me, in fact he did it. Then he limped round and did it the other side. He straightened up and peered out across the bush, looking for Kumina. He was still in sight, but only just. "Get in. We gotta go."

Slowly I got back behind the wheel. Wombley climbed in beside me.

There was no way I could follow Kumina except by driving over the bank of earth beside the road. It was about a metre high, maybe more, and quite steep. I decided to go at it straight. The front of the car went, like, straight up in the air in front of me and I thought we'd go over backwards. Wombley signalled, "Go back." So I let us roll back on to the road. Then he showed me I should go at it crooked.

When the front wheel on my side was halfway up the bank we were at such a steep angle I thought we were going to roll over, too! I was so scared my foot slipped down hard on the accelerator and – *whoomph!* – the Toyota suddenly sort of jumped forward with a roar like a pouncing panther. I felt the wheels kicking the sand back, and next second we were over the top and going much too fast down the other side, with the fallen truck coming straight towards us.

I thought for sure that we were going to crash into it. At the last moment, I swerved. I didn't think about it, I just did it. I drove around it and when we got to the other side I put the brakes on and sat there shaking.

"Hu-hooay! You good driver, Stacey." Wombley pointed the way. I just sat there. "Go along," he said, urging me.

"I don't want to. I can't. I'm scared." Frozen with terror, more like.

"You can easy do it, Stacey. You gotta do it." He was very calm, but very insistent.

"No."

We sat there for a long minute. I was quite determined

not to do it. He didn't say anything. And then he did say something.

"That bloke walking. It's Blue," he said.

I jolted upright. "Who?"

"It's your daddy."

My trembling stopped. Now I was frozen with something else. Something I can't describe. I suppose it was shock, with complete, total, utter surprise mixed in. Shock and surprise aren't the same. This was both together.

I turned to look at him. He was staring ahead, not at me.

"What do you mean?" I asked. My voice came out thin and fluttery.

"Your daddy was in Laverton. Now he's here."

I couldn't speak or even think. My dad – here? My dad was in that rolled-over motor?

"You said… he might be hurt. You said he might die."

"Yeah. We go along."

My hand acted by itself. It turned on the engine and I started driving into the bush.

When I think now how scared I was, that very first night, when Gran made me go off into the dark to fetch wood for the fire, how I was afraid of snakes and dingoes and even just of going to the loo when there wasn't one, and sleeping out under the stars, I can't believe it. Because that wasn't being

208

scared, not really, that was just *telling* myself I was scared. Working myself up over nothing.

Driving that four-by-four over no road, bumping over great lumps of spinifex so I thought we'd turn over, swerving to avoid rocks and dead branches, with Wombley pointing the way and Kumina coming in and out of sight ahead of us... *that* was scary. That was dangerous. I was cold with fear in all that heat. And blaming Dad, and yet at the same time, hungry to see him. Frightened for him. Because he must've been hurt when he rolled the truck. He just stumbled away into the bush. He couldn't have been that drunk. Nobody like him, who knew the bush, who'd grown up here, would do that unless they'd hit their head and were half out of it.

"How do you know it's him?" I asked Wombley.

"That's 'is tracks," said Wombley.

I was just gobsmacked. After all the years my dad had been away, Wombley still recognised his tracks.

But then of course he knew he was here. He must've heard he'd come back. Gran'd told me that Aborigines know everything that goes on. That was what Wombley meant, that day in the hospital. He was asking me if I'd seen Dad in town.

What was he doing here?

The answer came straight off. He was running away from whatever trouble he'd got into. He was running home to his mother. Where'd he got the money for the fare? And to buy a ute? God! Not from Mum! Surely not from Mum! Where would she get her hands on that kind of money?

But she'd do it somehow. If he asked her. I knew she would.

We drove through that hot, rough, bumpy, lonely bush for about half an hour. Of course after the first spurt to catch Kumina up, we were going very slowly, no faster than he could trot. But I had to watch the way every second, and keep swerving to avoid things, keeping my foot steady on the accelerator and ready to brake and turn. Sometimes I couldn't drive directly after Kumina because the going was too rough. Then I had to find a way round. Once I got lost and only Wombley kept me turning the right way. I stayed in first gear but still I was terrified. My insides were in a knot and I don't think I took one deep breath. My mouth was as dry as paper because it was open the whole time. The sweat was running into my eyes but I dared not take my hands off the wheel to wipe it. They were gripping it as if it would tear out of my hands and the car would go wild if I let it go.

I thought that journey would never, ever end.

But of course it did. At last we came around some trees and saw Kumina just ahead of us. He was holding a long thin man under the arms and dragging him towards a bit of shade made by a mulga. The man was my dad, sure enough.

It was really him. Even from a distance, and with the sun in my eyes, I could see it was him.

I put the brakes on and jumped out. The sun hit me like a mallet but I didn't feel it, apart from nearly falling over, but that was probably tension – my knees were wobbly. I ran over to the tree and knelt down beside my dad. Then I jumped up again quick, because the ground was so hot. Wombley took off his T-shirt and laid it down for me to sit on.

The first thing I noticed was that Dad didn't have a hat on. Even I knew that was dangerous. It must've fallen off when the truck rolled. He'd been out in the sun for hours without a hat. His face was burnt red and so was his scalp through his hair.

The second thing was the bump and the blood on his head. A lot of dried blood.

He wasn't quite unconscious. He was groaning. I took his head in my lap. There was a build-up of pressure in my chest. Despite everything, despite *everything*, this was actually a very special, wonderful moment in my life that I shall never forget. I remember every detail, even the pattern that the mulga shadow made on my dad's poor red hurt face. But what I remember most was the rush of love and happiness I felt when I held him. Just for that time it made all my bad feelings about him go away.

After just a minute, though, of feeling this love rushing through me, I had to do something. Wombley was handing me the water bottle. I splashed some on my top and tried to wipe Dad's face with it, but I couldn't, not while I was wearing it. I just had to do it with my hand. And after I'd splashed and wiped a few times he opened his eyes and stared up at me.

"I gotta have a drink," he said in a weak, croaky voice.

I could see he didn't know me. I poured some water into his mouth, and he gulped, and grabbed at the bottle, but then Wombley shook his head at me.

"Little bit," he said. "Too much make him sick up." So I poured a little more into his mouth, had a drink myself – God, I needed it! – and then gave the bottle back to Wombley.

"Gimme a drink!" Dad said, a bit louder.

"No, Dad, you mustn't."

His face changed. He'd taken me in.

"Stacey?"

"Yeah, it's me."

He shook his head and closed his eyes. Then he opened them again.

"It *is* you," he said. "Am I seeing things?"

"No."

"You – you're different."

"Well, you haven't seen me for two years," I said, trying really hard to sound reasonable and not choked up, which I was.

He tried to sit up, but his head hurt so much he had to lie down again.

I looked up at Wombley. "What shall I do?"

"Take 'im home."

I nodded. Kumina came close and between us we got Dad to his feet and helped him to the Toyota. Kumina was going to put him in the front next to me, but I stopped him.

"No, in the back. I need Wombley in the front to guide me. Here, put my hat on him."

They did it. Kumina got in the back with Dad. He took the water bottle and I saw him in the driving mirror, giving Dad little sips. I started driving.

I wasn't so scared this time. I think I was so full of other feelings I couldn't feel my fear. Or perhaps I was getting better at it. Wombley didn't talk. He sat well away from me, pushed right up against the door, and all he did was point the way. It didn't seem too long before we were back on the road and I pushed down on the accelerator and did a Gran, racing for home.

Chapter Twelve

When we drove into the yard, I saw Gran waiting. One look at her, even from a distance, and I knew it was me, not her, that was going to get the curry.

Before we'd even come close, she started jumping up and down, yelling like a madwoman.

"*Stacey!* Are you out of your *tree*? How dare you take the car? Are you trying to get yourself *killed*?"

I put the brake on and Wombley climbed stiffly out of the front seat. When she saw him, she lost it completely. I thought she was going to hit him.

"Wombley, if this is your doing I'll give you a good flogging with my crowbar, so help me God I will!"

I jumped out of the car. "Just look who's in the back before you shout at me, or him, Gran!" I yelled right back.

She stopped with her mouth open. Then she dashed up to the Toyota and peered into the back. I heard her gasp.

"My God, it's Darren," she whispered.

After that she turned and ran into the house, shouting for Dave. Between us me and Kumina lowered Dad down off the back and helped him to the foot of the veranda steps. Dave came out looking dazed. I thought at the time he'd just come-to after his drinking bout, but later I found out different.

He picked up my dad and carried him, all six feet of him, as if he didn't weigh hardly anything, into the house. Gran turned and looked at Wombley and Kumina. Her face had changed. It'd gone sort of grey under the tan, it sagged, and she looked suddenly very old. She moved her hands in a sign. I thought it meant "sorry" but she didn't say it. She said, "Thanks, fellas."

Then she said, "Where's your motor?"

Wombley pointed with his chin. "Close up."

Gran said, "Wait there. I'll get Dave to give you a lift."

Then she beckoned to me. I went to her and she put her arms round me.

"Where was he?"

"Out bush, Gran. He'd rolled his motor."

"You drove through the bush?" I nodded. She stared at me like she'd never looked at me properly. Then she sighed from down deep.

"You did a good job. Come on. Let's go see what your dad's been up to."

What could I say? Not a thing. I was *sorry* for her, losing her temper like that and then having to back down, even if she hadn't exactly said sorry. I actually found myself walking into the house holding hands with her. My kidnapper. But all that didn't seem a priority now. Dad, my no-good loser of a dad, was the priority.

Dave had laid Dad out on the double bed in Gran's room. Dad was a bit more awake. Dave fetched a basin of water and a cloth and started washing the blood away. Me and Gran stood over Dad and looked down at him. He opened his eyes a bit and said, "Hi, Ma."

"I'll hi-Ma you," she said. "What are you doing here?"

"I came home, Ma." He grinned at her, weakly and hopefully.

"Yeah, right," she said sarkily. "May one ask, where from?"

"London."

"Oh. What happened to Thailand? Or should I say, what happened *in* Thailand?"

He closed his eyes. "I can't talk about it now, Ma. My head's splitting." After a minute he opened them again and looked at me. "Ma, what's Stacey doing here?"

"Visiting me. Any objections?"

"Course not. Fair dinkum. I couldn't hardly believe it when I saw her out there. I thought I'd died and gone to heaven."

"That'll be the day! What heaven'd have you?"

He closed his eyes again. "Don't be hard, eh? This is heaven to me. Being back here. It feels so safe. I've missed you, Ma." I thought I saw a tear in the corner of his eye.

She muttered something under her breath that sounded like, "That's a good one." I gave her a nudge and scowled at her. Then I sat down on the edge of the bed and took his hand. He looked at me and squeezed my hand and we just stared at each other through our same-coloured eyes. When I was little he used to call me Sky Eyes.

He'd changed. It was hard to notice under his burnt skin, but he'd got older. He'd lost some hair. He had some wrinkles, and dark circles under his eyes. I could see he'd been through a bad time. Even if it *was* his own fault, I couldn't help feeling a bit sorry for him.

"Where's Mum?" I asked.

"I left her in England. She's been terrific. Like the Rock of Gibraltar. I'd never've got away without her help."

Oh. So she *had* raised the money for his fare. Bang went her bit in the Post Office Savings, everything we had in the flat that could be sold, probably including the *furniture*, and no doubt Nan had been made to chip in as well. My being sorry for him faded. But oddly enough, my feeling of loving him didn't.

Dave was rubbing some white cream on Dad's skin. Gran said, "Let Stace do that. You go and give the fellas all the meat we've got in the fridge, and see if you can start their truck. It probably just needs a push. Or if not, drive 'em into Cosmo. Get Harvey to send someone out to tow their truck back."

Dave hadn't said a word since we'd got back. Now he kind of growled, "Don't give me orders, I know what to do." I'd never heard him talk to her like that, and I wanted to ask him what was wrong, but he just put the jar of cream into my hands and stamped out of the room. It was while I was smearing the cream on to Dad's face, making him wince, that the idea came to me that Dave might have been getting curry from Gran before we got back. Who else would she have to yell at when she discovered the Toyota gone, and me with it?

"Were you mad at Dave about me taking the Toyota?" I asked.

"Too right I was!"

"It wasn't his fault. It was me decided to go."

"Not his fault? Laying there pissed as a maggot leaving you on your own? Anything could've happened!"

"Well, whose fault was it he got pissed?"

"Don't say 'pissed', Stacey," she said. Then she did a double take. "You're not saying it was my fault, I hope!"

"Yes I am."

I finished putting on the cream. Dad had sort of fallen asleep, at least his eyes were closed again, but I didn't want to talk in front of him, so I said, "Let's leave him to rest now."

We went out. The minute she'd closed the door, she said, "I want to know what you meant."

"He told me."

"What?"

"That you don't plan to send me home."

She sat down suddenly on the sofa.

There was a long silence. She didn't look at me. It was like she was figuring out what to say to me. In the end, she looked up and said, "That's right, Stacey." She was looking me right in the eye.

All my hot, furious words that I'd got ready hours ago had gone. But some of the anger was still there. I said, "But how could you?"

"Stacey, ask yourself. What would I be sending you back to?"

"Home, that's what."

"That lousy little council flat—"

"Thanks! It was good enough for you to plonk yourself in for five weeks, anyway! You never thought you might be in the way, making me move out of my room!"

"Do you think I didn't think of that? I was mortified. But I had to be ruthless! I had to see how things were. If I hadn't been living with you, you could've pulled the wool over my eyes, pretended things were OK. As it was, I soon saw how you were fixed, poor as bush rabbits and your mum working her fingers to the bone, smoking fit to bust a lung and hardly ever at home, and you not trying hard enough at school… What would you have done when your mum nicked off, if I hadn't have been right there to give you some TLC?"

"I'd have managed on my own!"

"Yeah? You should've seen yourself when you got that note. Fourteen-year-old kids can't live on their own."

"Maybe Mum wouldn't have gone, if you hadn't been there for backup! Did you ever think of *that*?"

"With women like her, their man comes first and the kids come a poor second. I bet she'd have left that note and gone running after him, whether I'd been there or not."

I didn't answer. I was suddenly *burning* with loyalty for my mum. I *knew* she wouldn't leave me for ever. No matter what. But still, there was some truth in what Gran was saying and I knew it. She had nicked off, after all, and she hadn't phoned me for three whole days.

"And look at the thanks she gets!" Gran went on. "Her fella may think she's the Rock of Gibraltar, he may pin medals all over her, but that hasn't stopped him nicking off again and leaving her. And instead of telling him to go stew in his own juice, I bet she's sitting alone at home congratulating herself on having done her wifely duty."

I thought it was a lot more likely she was sitting alone crying her eyes out. And no one to give *her* any TLC. I remembered the scrappy little note I'd left her. *Bye, Mum, I'm off to Aussie-land with Gran for Christmas! See you when I get back*. And now, if I couldn't do something about it, I wasn't bloody well *going* back, and she'd be all on her tod for keeps. No Dad, no me, no money – no furniture maybe. God! I had to get back. I had to!

And now, I thought I could. Because, from the minute I'd set eyes on him, somewhere in the bottom of my mind had been this thought: *Gran's the mamu who's stolen me and Dad's going to rescue me. I'm falling out of the tree and he's going to catch me and take me home*.

Everything calmed down after Dave took off with Wombley and Kumina. Dad was asleep in a shuttered room. Gran was kind of zonked out after all the stress and yelling. There wasn't much for me to do except go and find my little Roo and maybe feed the emus. They hadn't been around when I'd done the chooks. I thought they must be really hungry by now, and when they got hungry they always came into the yard from wherever they hung out the rest of the time.

Roo wasn't in her pillowcase.

I looked all round the place for her. She was getting more independent now and she often hopped about, hoovering up any scraps of food or grain she could find, but then if I wasn't around she'd hop back into her "pouch". Only now I couldn't find her.

At first I wasn't worried. What could happen to her? She could get out of the yard and run away, but I didn't think she was ready to do that. She was still my baby.

I put my anti-snake boots on and went out of the yard and began to walk round the whole homestead in a big circle, calling her. I wasn't too worried about snakes any more, I knew how to look out for them. I walked on open bits of ground and left the big tufts of spinifex and bits of junk and wood alone. But there was one chunk of wood that got in my way, and I kicked it aside. That was when I found what was left of Nora and Dora, AKA Loretta and Merinda.

Big emu feathers, in a drift where they'd blown under the wood, about a hundred metres behind the house. Not many. But there was blood on the ground too. I knew straight off they'd been killed.

I stood there, like, *stunned*. Who would do it? A mob, of course, who else? There was no one else. Not Wombley and Kumina's lot, it couldn't have been them. Some other mob.

I forgot Roo for the moment and rushed back into the house.

"Gran! Someone's killed our emus!"

"*What!*"

She jumped up and came running after me, picking up her boots on the way. She fell behind a bit, struggling to get into them as she came down the steps, but she soon caught me up. I led her round and showed her. She stood there staring down, and then she just burst into tears.

I'd never seen her cry before. It was horrible. Whether she was her dressed-up city self or her tough outback self, I'd never thought she could cry like that. I put my arms around her and hugged her.

"Don't cry, Gran! Please don't. We'll find out who did it. Oh, please don't be so upset!" It made me feel all wobbly and insecure inside to see her really roaring-crying like a little girl.

"Those rotten murderers!" she howled.

"They probably just hunted them, they didn't know they were your pet ones."

"Didn't know! Of course they bloody knew! Do you think wild emus are as well fed as Nora and—" But when she tried to say their names, she started crying harder than ever. "They've thrown them in the fire and burnt their feathers off and roasted them and they're eating them right

223

this minute, the miserable mongrels! After all the favours I've done them! And there's not a thing I can do about it!"

"Can't you report it?"

"The Wonngais have hunting rights all over this area. It doesn't matter if they shot them right on my doorstep, not if they had placards round their necks with 'Don't shoot me, I'm Glendine's pet!' on 'em! Oh, dammit, dammit, dammit, my poor babies!"

I led her into the house and poured her a beer. She was shaking and heaving with sobs.

"Lubly fat ones, that's what they'd say…" she muttered through her tears.

And of course then I remembered Kumina saying that about Roo. I felt shock run all over me like ice water.

"Gran! I can't find Roo. You don't think—?"

She stared at me through her tears with her mouth open. "They wouldn't dare," she breathed. "They couldn't! They know I'd skin them alive if they touched your… No. No. She's too small. They don't often kill the little ones for food, they wait till they're bigger. Don't, Stace, don't be frightened. We'll find her."

"Kumina said he'd like to eat her!"

"Kumina was teasing you, he wouldn't do that. Anyway, he was with you." She wiped her eyes and blew her nose. "Come on. Let's go and look for her."

There was only about half an hour of daylight left. We just abandoned Dad and hunted for Roo, circling the homestead, calling. We didn't find her. I was gutted. I couldn't even cry. I wanted Roo so badly and I was so scared for her, I was all frozen up. Funny word to use when we were half baked to death in the heat.

When the sun went down we went back into the house. Gran had her arm around me but I felt too bad for comfort. Roo was dead. I just knew she was.

"Go and look in on your dad," she said.

I did. A bit late, I felt guilty for leaving him. But he was still asleep. I sat on the bed beside him and thought how I wanted him to wake up and hold me in his arms and take charge. But he didn't. So I went to my bedroom and lay down, and stayed like that for another long while, just, like, wiped out with misery, until I heard the Toyota drive into the yard. I heard Gran and Dave talking, then Dave came into my room without knocking.

"I hear you lost Roo," he said. "Well here's what. I'm going to drive back out to the road, and wait. Harvey, at Cosmo, will have Wombley's motor on the road in no time. Then they'll be driving back up by here to meet up with the rest of their mob. And I'll put them on to it. If any of their mob has dared take Roo, Wombley'll find out, and if she's still alive, he'll bring her back."

"But they killed Nora and Dora!"

"Well, someone did," he said grimly. "But they killed 'em for food. If they took Roo, I'm saying *if*, it's more likely to have been for one of their kids to play with. They know she's tame… I doubt if they've killed her."

I thought of Kumina, in the dark by the hospital, holding her in both hands and opening his mouth wide… and I did cry. I cried like Gran. Dave came and sat on the bed and let me cry on him and gave me a cuddle. "Don't, chookie," he said. "We'll get her back, trust me we will."

What made me cry harder and longer was that Dave was being more of a dad to me than my dad was.

Chapter Thirteen

So Dave went off in the Toyota, into the dark, and me and Gran started to make tea. Dad was still asleep.

"Gran, shouldn't you call the Flying Doctor for Dad?"

"He's OK."

"But that bump on his head!"

"It's nothing. He'll be fine."

"But he was out in the sun so long! Shouldn't we wake him up and give him water?"

She sighed. "Let sleeping mongrels lie," she said.

"Gran! How can you be so mean about him, he's your son!"

"Let *him* remember that. Some other time than when he's in trouble." But she followed me into the bedroom. Dad was stirring in the dark.

"Well, Darren, how are you feeling?" she asked, all nursey, not like a mum.

"Crook," he said. She put her hand on his forehead.

"No fever," she said. "Still got a headache?"

"It's a bit better. Not much."

"Feel like getting up for tea?"

"Maybe," he said in a stronger voice. "What is it?"

Gran said, really short, "Get up and see."

He got up slowly. He staggered a bit and clutched me.

"Thanks, Sky Eyes," he said. "I'm real glad you're here."

"Are you, Dad?"

"Oh, I know what you're thinking."

"Do you?"

"Yeah, but don't be hard on me." I wished he'd stop saying that.

We went into the living room with him leaning on my arm.

"Got an aspirin or something, Ma?"

Gran gave him a couple of paracetamols with a glass of water. "Drink it slowly now."

"Or you'll sick up," I said, remembering Wombley.

Dad sat down on the sofa. "It's so good to be back," he said again. But he had this way of rolling his eyes up at Gran kind of like a dog that thinks it's going to get punished.

"So what happened in Thailand?" Gran said.

"Ma, don't get after me."

"There's two people here you owe an explanation to."

Dad drooped his head. He looked so miserable. I put my arm around him. "Let him alone, Gran, eh?" I said.

He smiled at me sideways. He has this lovely smile. "D'you still love your old dad, Stacey?" he asked. But Gran was having none of it.

"Oh, fair go, don't give her that mush!" she snapped. "You left her and her mother flat, and now you've turned up here because you've nowhere else to go, so don't start working for the sympathy vote! Cut the bull and tell us what happened."

Dad kept sipping water. I thought he was doing it to put off talking.

"Have a heart, Ma," he said at last. "Don't make me drag it all out in front of Stacey. I'll tell you, but not her. I can't and that's the truth."

I got up. "I'll get on with the tea," I said. I thought it was the nicest thing I could do for him right now.

While I was cooking omelettes in the kitchen I could hear Dad's voice going on, very quietly. I couldn't make out any words but I didn't want to. As much as I'd liked Gran's Christmas story about how he'd taken her out to dinner, I didn't think I'd like to hear about the trouble the slapper had landed him in, or what he'd done to get out of it.

When the omelettes were ready I turned the heat off and went out the back way with the big torch. I wanted Roo. It was like an ache in my chest. I crept round the front of the house to see if by a miracle she was in her pillowcase on the veranda, but she wasn't. Then I just wandered around the yard feeling empty and sad. My dad was here, and he felt crook and was in trouble. It would be awful if I felt worse about my pet roo being missing, probably dead, than I felt about him.

I sat in the shade house in the dark and thought about whether I wanted to go home or not. I had wanted to, before Dad came. Not just for my mum's sake. Because it was home and what I was used to. But now I wasn't so sure. It was good here with Gran and Dave. And now Dad was here. I had two parents, after all, and this one seemed to need me too. To be on his side, especially if Gran was against him. It was like a movie when the heroine is pulled two ways, which is fun to watch, but not when the heroine is you.

I kept interrupting my thoughts to think about Dave, sitting out in the dark by the road, waiting for Wombley and Kumina to drive by. I wished he'd come back. I went and stood at the yard gate for a few minutes and flashed the torch about. Then I went back in the house.

Gran met me in the kitchen. She looked sort of ill. Grey in the face again and sweating a bit. It must've been bad, what Dad told her. I suppose I'm a coward, because I was glad I hadn't had to listen. My idea is, the slapper set him up as some kind of a male mule – that's a drug carrier – and then ditched him when she thought the cops were on to him.

"Tea ready?" was all she said.

"Cold by now. What'd he say?"

She shut the door.

"Stacey, I'd tell you everything, but he's asked me not to. And maybe that's better. You and he need to talk, but don't try to drag everything out of him. That girl made a real mug of him and he knows it now. You don't want to shame him, do you?" I didn't say anything and she didn't look at me. After a minute she said, "Everybody makes mistakes," and I saw she was crying again. But she pulled herself out of it.

The three of us sat down at the table and I served the omelettes. Dad asked if I'd made them. "Fair dinkum," he said. "You're a great cook, possy." (That was his other nickname for me. Nicknames seem to run in the family.)

After tea Gran left us to wash up together. It was a bit obvious that she was leaving us alone.

"Do you feel OK?" I asked.

"Not so dusty," he said. "Ma told me how you rescued me."

"It was Wombley and Kumina really."

"Good old Wombley. Still my mate. He used to call me Blue."

"He still does."

"But you did the driving. There's no two ways about it, possy, you saved my life. Another hour laying out there in the sun and I'd have been food for the buzzards."

I washed. He dried. After a while I said, "I've got something to tell you."

"Yeah? What?"

"Well, Gran brought me here, and now she's saying she's not going to send me back."

"What do you think about that?"

He didn't seem surprised. It must have come out when they were talking.

"I think it's pretty rotten of Gran. Don't you? I mean, it's kidnapping."

"She's doing it for your own good."

"Don't you think I should have some say in it?"

"You're only a kid, possy."

"Yes, and you're my dad. You can tell her to let me go back and she'd have to."

His hands on the dishcloth stopped. He was frowning as if this was a new idea.

"You've left Mum alone at home," I pushed on. "I ought to go back and be with her, right?"

"Unless you'd rather stay here with Ma and me."

"You think that'd be OK?"

"Well – it's one way to go."

"Let's say I want to go home. What are you going to do about it?"

"About what?"

"*Dad.* About Gran. Wanting to keep me here."

He dried another plate slowly. I stopped washing. I waited. I hardly breathed. I knew, then, at the time, that this was a key moment.

He sighed.

"Well," he said, "I just don't know what I can do about it."

I turned and looked at him. He gave me one quick look back, then turned away. I knew then it was hopeless. He wouldn't help. He couldn't. He couldn't stand up to her. He never had. She was a strong character and he wasn't, and that was probably why he'd run away from her in the first place. *And* why he'd run back when it all got too much for him.

It was all getting too much for *me.* I started out of the room.

"Stacey?"

I stopped with my back to him. I couldn't look him in the face. I didn't want him to see what I was thinking.

"There's something…" He'd dropped his voice really low. "Your mum said that when Ma was with you in London, she seemed to be loaded."

"Yeah. So?"

"But I don't get it. She's always been dead broke. She hasn't got a cracker. She never has had."

I turned around. "Of course she has. Her rich husband left it to her, the one with the big house in Melbourne."

"What gave you that idea? He left his money to his kids from his first wife. He didn't leave her a thin dollar. Just a half-share of the house. She sold it to come back here and start up again with more cattle."

I couldn't take it in. "So… where did she get all that money she spent in London? All the clothes? Bringing me here?"

"That's what I want to know."

At that moment I heard Dave driving into the yard. I forgot everything and dashed out the front door and jumped down the steps just as he was getting out of the Toyota. I sort of ran right into him and nearly knocked him over. He grabbed me to steady me.

"Sorry, chook, I haven't got her, but don't give up hope. When I told Wombley you'd lost her, you know what he did, he turned right around and started driving back to Cosmo. That must mean something, even though he didn't say much."

My heart kind of bounced. "So she could still be alive!"

"Course she could."

"Thanks, Dave. You're a real – mate. Come in and have some tea."

I found myself hugging his arm as we went up the steps. Dad came out on to the veranda and saw us. His face went funny. I took my arm out of Dave's, quick.

We all sat round the table and I made Dave a fresh omelette while he had some beer. Dad wanted one too but Gran said no and made him go on with the water. Dave bolted his tea and then pushed his plate away and said, "OK, now we have to talk about Stacey going home."

The rest of us stiffened and sat up straight, even Dad. Gran glared at Dave.

"This is none of your business. Keep your nose out," she said in a warning voice.

"If she's going to catch her flight on Tuesday we have to start for Perth tomorrow."

"How do you know her flight's on Tuesday?"

"Come on, woman," said Dave, "how do you think I know?"

"You've been stickybeaking into my wallet," said Gran, and now she definitely sounded dangerous.

Dave didn't deny it. He reached for another can of beer and popped it open. He didn't seem at all bothered now

235

about Gran being mad at him. He just sat there, calmly waiting to see what else she'd say.

"I'm tearing that ticket up. She's not going back!" she said, all fierce.

"Don't you think that might be Stacey's call?" Dave said, really quietly.

Gran looked flustered. You didn't often see her looking flustered. It was Dave standing up to her that was doing it, you could see that with one eye shut.

I decided to join in. It was me they were talking about after all. It was *my life*.

"I might not *want* to go home," I said. "I like it here now. But there's Mum. Someone's got to be with her. And I have to go to school," I remembered. "It was you who said that was a priority, Gran."

"Don't you worry about that!" said Gran. I could tell she was furious with all of us. "Of course you've got to learn. You can do School of the Air, through the radio, like other kids on stations do!"

"WHAAAT!" I shouted. "Learn at home with no teacher!"

"I could teach you—"

"No you couldn't, Gran! I couldn't learn from you! I want to be with other kids, I need proper teachers like I have at home!"

"You told me they were no good."

"They're better than nothing! At least they make you get your head down. If I was here with all the distractions, I'd never learn a thing. I told you how lazy and useless I am, I have to be *made* to work!"

"Too right," said Dave. "Human nature."

Gran was staring at me as if I was a chook who'd jumped off the ground and pecked her. Dad seemed to feel he ought to say something.

"Well, I think she should stop here," he said.

"I'd keep my trap shut if I was you, mate," said Dave.

"Who the hell d'you think you're talking to?"

"I'm talking to you. You got no rights, you gave 'em up when you left her. Keep out of it."

There was a silence. A *horrible* silence. Then Dad's sunburnt face suddenly turned purple. He picked up a full can of beer and threw it at Dave's head.

Dave's hand flew up and he caught it in midair. He jumped up, and drew back his hand as if he was going to bash Dad in the face with the can. Dad jerked backwards and his chair went over and he landed on the floor with a crash. Gran and I both shouted at once and rushed to help him. His legs were sticking up in the air and he looked silly. I pulled the chair free and he lay on his back, groaning.

Gran took Dad's head in her lap. She cradled him. I knelt by him and held his hand. We were both making more fuss than when he first arrived. I think I was crying. Gran was saying things like "Lovie, are you all right?" and at last her voice sounded like a mum's. She turned on Dave.

"Leave him alone!" she said. "He's in no condition! He's only doing what's right as her father!"

"Oh. Her father, now, is he?" said Dave. "Bit late for that, isn't it?"

Dad was climbing to his feet with one hand rubbing his back. "Who the hell is this old mongrel, anyway?"

"I've looked after your old cheese for ten years, so I have some rights around here," Dave said. "And I wouldn't mind betting I can look after Stacey better than you ever did."

"I looked after her for twelve years!" shouted Dad. "You've only known her a couple of weeks! If you weren't an old codger I'd punch your lights out!"

"You're on," said Dave. "Come outside."

Things were getting unbearable. And it was all because of me. I had to try and stop it.

"Shut up, *both* of you!" I yelled. They looked at me with surprised faces. "I'll decide this!"

Dave said, "That's my chook."

I had one more lightning think. There's a trick I've sometimes done with little things, at home, when I haven't

238

been able to make up my mind. I've wiped my brain clear and let the first yes or no that came into it, decide. I did that now.

I took a deep breath when the answer came flashing in.

"I've got to go home and that's the end of it! Now who's going to drive me to Perth tomorrow?"

Chapter Fourteen

Of course, that wasn't the end of the discussion (row). Gran didn't just give in. But when Dad switched sides, she knew she was licked, and coughed up my return ticket and passport (which, in case you want to know, she'd hidden under the lino-stuff on the kitchen floor. It didn't look exactly new any more, it was filthy from people walking on it). So it was settled.

I went to bed early. I was, like, totally knackered. Dave went to bed early too, because he was going to drive me to Perth – Gran refused to. It was her last stand, she said she'd have nothing to do with sending me back, that she'd as soon send me to Outer Siberia as back to Peckham.

I'd more or less packed before. I lugged my case in from the veranda and stuffed the last bits in. The only thing left out now was my emu egg. I didn't know how to be sure it wouldn't get broken, so in the end I wrapped it in two T-shirts and stuffed it (carefully) in my hand luggage. Then there was nothing for me to do except get into bed (or on to bed, no sheet even) and lie awake thinking. And listening. What I listened to, apart from the usual night noises from outside, was Gran and Dad talking. They talked and talked and talked as if they had fifteen years' worth of catching up to do. Yeah, right. They did.

So I was sort of free of worrying about Dad because I could tell Gran's coldness to him had cracked when he fell over backwards at the table. It'd probably been kind of thawing out slowly ever since she first saw him, but she'd had fifteen years to freeze up and I suppose that can't defrost all in a minute. Gran was two people all right, not just a got-up city type and a bushie Gran, but a nice person and a not so nice one. Well – like most people. The nice side of her had come out quite quickly, considering all those years when she hadn't hardly heard from him. Now I could hear how her voice was all quiet and gentle through my bedroom wall. She was going to look after him and that meant I needn't.

So instead I thought about Wombley and Kumina, and Merinda and Alexis, and poor Nora and Dora being eaten like the Christmas bustard. I thought of the chooks and Humpy Not-so-White and even Spotty (though I never got

241

to know her much, but I did help fix her windmill). There was nothing in my thoughts to cheer me up because I was so sad to leave them all.

I let my mind stretch out across the bush with its red earth and twisty mulga trees and medicine-smelling gums and big bluey-green clumps of spinifex. I had no camera and no way to take it home with me except in my memory – oh, and in my notepad, of course. That was half-full already and I could write more on the plane. I thought of my Epic Drive, which I hadn't written about yet. I felt really, really proud of myself for doing that. Actually, thinking about the whole time I'd been here, I was only ashamed of the beginning when I acted so wussy. I felt I hadn't done badly on the whole. And tonight, when I'd stood up to them and stopped the men fighting, and made my own decision – I felt that'd been pretty good, too. I didn't remember ever feeling so good about myself.

I had my kidnapper to thank for all that. Weird or what? Maybe it was Grandma Glendine's genes that gave me a bit of gumption (Nan's favourite word).

I didn't think about Dave much. I know it's stupid but I seemed to love Dave more than anyone and be saddest to leave him, but I knew I'd have hours of driving to be with him and say goodbye to him in my heart.

When I kept not being able to sleep, I knew I had to say goodbye to something else. Like, here. So I got out of bed and put my boots on, and went outside very quietly, out the back. I stood out there under the stars. I was naked except for my boots, and I felt that was right. Nothing between me and all of it. I thought about people who believe that heaven's in the sky somewhere. I don't know how they can believe that now there are satellites and spaceships and stuff up there, but there's something wonderful and mysterious about the sky, that's for sure. I looked for my mubrun – my totem scorpion. I found him after a bit (he'd moved a little). He was so bright and beautiful with his great curvy tail. I said goodbye silently to him and promised to look for him in the English sky, and if I couldn't find him, keep him inside me like that crazy goanna in Merinda's story (only in my head, not my doony!). Then I went back to bed feeling better. Maybe that's what your mubrun's supposed to do for you.

My last thought before I fell asleep in the hot darkness was about Roo. I'd been pushing thoughts of her away. Maybe Wombley would bring her back in the morning. But then I'd have to say goodbye to her, too. That sounds as if I didn't hope she was alive. It was just I couldn't imagine parting from her.

We were supposed to start early next day, and I'd set my inner clock to wake me at five. I can always do that, unless it's for school. That was even earlier than I had to get up, because I wanted to do something. I wanted to try to draw the homestead, to have just one picture to take home with me.

I dressed and sneaked out the back way so as not to wake Dave and Gran with the squeaking screen door. I took the stool from the wash house and walked round to the front and right out to the gate where I could get a panoramic view of the place, with the windmill and the trees and the shade house and everything. It was just starting to get light. All the shadows and silhouettes around the horizon were just beginning to show. I smelt the air and tried to make a memory of that special smell of dust and chooks and gum leaves and other things I still had no names for.

And I just sat there for half an hour as the sun came up and sketched what I could see in pencil into my notepad. I must say for someone who gets Ds in art it wasn't bad. (It's in front of me right now as I write this. I tore it off the pad and bought a clip frame for it.)

I was just finishing when someone sounded a horn behind me and nearly made me jump out of my skin.

Gran and Dave were still asleep on the forty-fours. Into the yard came a ute with a white man sitting in front. I ran across and shook Gran awake.

"Gran, someone's here."

244

She woke up straight away and swung her legs down. Just as she was climbing off the platform, the man got out of the car. He was dressed in jeans and a big leather hat.

Gran was getting into some kind of dressing gown thing in a big hurry. (*She* didn't sleep in the raw, luckily. She had some shorty pyjamas on.)

"Joe," she said, not sounding at all pleased. "What's going on?"

Dave was waking up now. He was leaning on his elbow on the platform, looking at this new person.

"Do you two know each other?" he asked.

"Joe," said Gran. "From the mining company."

Dave sat up, frowning, and got off the platform the other side. "I'm going in," he said.

"Put the kettle on," said Gran. "Stacey, go and get breakfast started."

I followed Dave into the house. He went into the kitchen with me after him. "Who is he?" I asked.

"Search me. The mining company are doing some exploring about 10 k up the road from here. I've been out to check up on 'em a couple of times. Dunno what they're sniffing around for. Cheeky mongrel, coming at sparrowfart like this."

He put the kettle on and I put out some stuff for breakfast. Gran came in with this Joe. She looked a bit – I don't know exactly. Uneasy. She certainly wasn't looking Dave in the eye.

"Dave, can you come a minute," she said in a very small voice, and Dave followed her into my room. Gran closed the door after them.

Joe took his hat off and stood there awkwardly, turning it in his hands. We didn't say anything. Then Dad came in from Gran's bedroom where he'd slept, rubbing his eyes, half-dressed. The two men sort of nodded to each other and I poured them two mugs of coffee. Nobody was speaking when we all heard Dave shout "WHAT! You did WHAT!" and we heard Gran say "Shhhh!"

"I'll give you shush, woman!" Dave yelled. He came bursting back in, his face all red. He marched straight up to Joe. "You better believe it, I knew nothing about this," he said. "It's all news to me. Until I get my head around it, you better get back to the camp. I'll come and see you in a few days."

"This is a pretty serious business," said Joe. "The boss had to go to Perth, but he sent me to sort it out. I wouldn't want to go back empty handed. He'd have my guts for garters."

Dave rubbed his hand over his head. "I can't talk about this now," he said. "I've got a plane to catch."

"We need to talk about it now. There's quite a lot involved here."

"How much?"

"Well, it's not just the money. We think there's something sus about the whole deal."

"I'm asking you. How much did you loan her?"

"Er – I wouldn't call it a loan exactly, but it was thirty thousand dollars."

I thought Dave was going to pass out. He closed his eyes and kind of reeled. Then he pulled himself together.

"Fair go, mate, there's got to be some mistake."

Joe shook his head. "'Fraid not."

"How could you possibly loan her so much?"

"Well, it was an option, see."

"An option? For what?"

"Oh…" He looked vague. "Just on spec, you know… I came along here one day – round about October, wasn't it, Glendine? – with the boss and told Glendine we'd like to do some drilling on her property. We paid her thirty thou to let us excise part of the station."

"Thirty thousand dollars *on spec*? You must've found something!"

"Well, yeah, maybe, some traces, you know… worth a gamble. Anyhow, we took out the option and were planning to start drilling on your south-east corner this month, and we'd done all the searches with our native advisers, like, in case there should be any sacred sites that would cause

247

trouble, and it was all dinkum until the Native Title Tribunal bloke came along last week and told us one of the local Abos—" Gran stiffened. He coughed and corrected himself quickly. "—Aborigines, had gone to them about some waterhole just where we were going to get set up, said it was a very important site for 'em, and now we're snookered. Can't touch it."

"So now you think you can have your money back?"

This was Gran. She'd drawn herself up straight and walked up to Joe, who backed away. She was taller than him.

"Yeah," said Joe.

"Whistle for it!" she said. "It's gone, I've spent it. It's not my fault if you didn't do your homework. Write it off as a bad debt and go and drill somewhere else."

"Well," said Joe, "that'd be one thing, if we hadn't done our homework, but we had. We know the score, we've had our fingers burnt before now with these so-called sacred sites. I'd like to settle this nicely, but we've got pretty strong evidence that somebody tipped off the local mob to go to the Native Title blokes. We found a witness who'll swear it was a setup. We think we've got a case, and if you dig your heels in, Glendine, I'm afraid we may have to take you to court."

Dave still seemed gobsmacked. "What are you suggesting? That Glendine took your money and then

248

tipped off one of the Cosmo mob to snooker you with the NTT?"

Joe looked uncomfortable. "I'd rather not say any more at this stage, in case it turns legal."

"Who's this 'witness' you're threatening us with? It couldn't be one of the Cosmo mob unless you bribed him!"

"I wouldn't start throwing accusations around if I was in your position," said Joe. He put his hat back on and started towards the door. "You'll be hearing from our lawyers," he said, and went out. A minute later we heard his ute start up and drive away.

There was a kind of stunned silence. Then Dave turned on Gran. "Why didn't you tell me, woman? You said you'd borrowed money from your sister!"

"Lally could only let me have five thousand. I knew you'd be against doing a deal with a mining company."

"Too right! If anybody's going to drill for gold on this spread, it'll be yours truly!"

He sat down and rubbed his hand all over his head again, as if it itched.

Then Dad spoke up. "Did you do what he hinted at?" he asked. He sounded sort of excited.

"No!" she said. They looked at her. "Well. Not exactly. I knew about the waterhole, Brando told me about it once and said I shouldn't go there."

"So you knew they couldn't drill there," said Dad.

"How was I to know exactly where they wanted to drill?"

"Because of course they told you," said Dave.

"Well, it's not my fault if I knew about the waterhole and they didn't."

"And you never even hinted to Brando what was in the wind? You never suggested he complain to the Native Title Tribunal?"

"Would I do a thing like that?" she said. "I only rang up directory assistance one time when I was in Laverton and got the number for him... But he did the talking to the lawyer," she finished, all innocent.

Dave and Dad stared at her. Then Dad burst out laughing. Dave kept staring at her, kind of helpless.

"I always knew you were a bit crazy," he said. "I didn't know you were a crook."

She went and sat by him at the table.

"Listen, Dave. Those mining companies are drowning in dough. Thirty thousand's nothing to them, and I needed it to go to London. They've swindled and tricked so many pastoralists like us out of parts of our stations – or even whole stations – they deserve to be outsmarted once in a while. You should've seen the way they talked to me, like I was some stupid little woman."

"Why didn't you tell me?"

"You'd have stopped me dealing with a mongrel like Joe, you know you would."

"I could almost feel sorry for the bloke," he said. "It's pretty obvious he's screwed up. His job's on the line... 'On spec', eh? Well, that's a lie, for a start. They found something. Something big. We may be sitting on a bloody fortune."

"Dave, don't get that look in your eye. I don't want you turning us into a mining outfit. Spotty would hate those dirty big digging machines making holes near one of her windmills and getting dust in her eyes."

Dave looked all around the room as if he was looking for help. When he got to me, he said, "I can't do this now. Come on, Stacey, we're going. Where's your luggage?" I pointed to my room. He went in, and came out again straight away with my big case and all my hand luggage. He didn't say a word to anybody, he just walked out the front.

I didn't know what to do. This wasn't the way I wanted to say goodbye. I went up to Dad first and kind of kissed him. He put one arm around me and gave me a hug, but he didn't say anything... couldn't meet my eye. Then I went to Gran. No hug from her. Just a very straight look.

"It's not too late to change your mind, Stace," she said. "I wish you would. Please do!"

"I can't, Gran."

It was all happening too quickly. Even after all my goodbye thoughts the night before, I wasn't ready. But I heard Dave sounding the horn on the Toyota. Two long, impatient blasts.

"I have to go," I said. I ran to the door, and then turned back. "Gran, if – if Wombley brings Roo back, will you look after her?"

She dropped down in a chair and put her face in her hands. She moved her head, but I couldn't tell if it was a nod or a shake. Just as I was leaving I saw Dad sit down beside her and put his arm round her.

So I went out and joined Dave, and we were just driving away, when – you may not believe this because it was so amazing – just as we were going out of the yard, we met a motor coming in. It was Wombley!

I jumped out of the Toyota before it even stopped and ran to the window. "Hi Wombley have you got her?" I yelled all in one breath.

He smiled and shook his head. But he quickly said, "She's not dead, Stacey." Like, to put me out of my suspense. "Merinda got her."

"Merinda!"

"Yeah. Merinda's cousin, he took her for Merinda. Merinda want to keep her but I said she couldn't. They bringin' her back today."

"But we're going," I said. "I'm leaving now. I'm going back to England."

Wombley didn't say anything. Dave had got out of the car too by now and he said, "Why didn't you bring her back?" Wombley said, "Rinda cryin' for her. She want to keep her."

I stood very still and thought about it.

"But she won't be safe with Merinda," I said.

Wombley said, "She be right, why not?"

"Because when she grows a bit, Kumina or someone will kill her to eat."

He shrugged. "When they grow they no good for pets."

"So you kill them?"

He shrugged again. It made perfect sense to him. But I wasn't having that.

"Merinda can keep her till she grows up," I said. "But then you have to bring her here. You must promise not to let anyone hurt her."

Dave said, "Are you really right with that, Stacey?"

I nodded. I wanted to cry but it was no use. Part of me'd known from the beginning that I'd have to give her up. And this wasn't so bad. Merinda would love her and take care of her. "It's better than just turning her loose to be hunted," I said.

And then Dave said, "We won't turn her lose. We'll take her to the wildlife park. She'll be safe and happy there."

Wombley looked relieved. I suppose Merinda had kicked up a fuss about giving her back and now Wombley didn't have to make her. He grinned a big white grin and nodded hard. "We bring her when she big, no worries," he said. "I tell Kumina she not for tucker."

Dave nodded to him. "You drove a long way. I'll give you a can of diesel to get back on."

He went to get it. While I was waiting, Dad came out.

"Hi there, Wombley."

"Blue."

"How you going? How's the leg?"

"She's right now."

I noticed they were using signs.

"Dad, what're the signs for 'thank you' and 'goodbye'?" I said.

He showed me and I did them both for Wombley. (I can still do them.) And then Gran came running.

"Stacey! Wait!" she called. My heart sank. She was going to start begging and asking me not to go again. But she didn't.

She said, "I just want to tell you. I like you for standing up for yourself, for not letting your mum down. You're a real Aussie now. You'll never be a doormat. Don't forget me, will you? And don't think too badly of me for trying to steal you."

"It's OK, Gran." It was a really soppy scene with us hugging but I was well glad she'd come out and said that. If Wombley hadn't shown up it wouldn't have happened, because we'd have been gone. And maybe I wouldn't have forgiven her because she hadn't asked me to.

Come to think of it, she still hadn't, not in so many words, but I forgave her anyway. After all, people only steal something if they really want it.

Well. Not counting Loretta and the lace knickers.

On the long, long way to Perth, Dave and I talked. You can talk a lot in fifteen hours. (We stopped for meals and a rest in a couple of the little towns on the way.)

The bits I remember were mainly about what was going to happen. Dave wasn't all that worried about the mining company maybe taking Gran to court. He said the worst they could do to her was sue her for the money back. He said the mining boss was a mongrel with a bad temper and he'd be so pissed off at being snookered by a woman, he just might do it. On the other hand, he might be *ashamed* of being snookered by a woman, and *not* do it. But what kept coming into the conversation was gold.

Dave kept thinking about it. He told me about a big mine called the Lady Bountiful. "They found four big chunks of gold, and a pipe that led down into an old channel, from prehistoric times, where there'd been a riverbed. Deep under the ground. The gold had washed down there and got compressed by all the weight of earth above it. It was white as beach sand, and so hard you couldn't break it with a 'dozer. Worth millions."

"I thought you hated mining."

"I hate mining for other people. I wouldn't mind if it was for me – I'm not stupid. I don't want to be bush-rabbit poor all my life."

"If you got rich, Gran could be the other Glendine again."

"What 'other Glendine'?"

So I told him about how she'd been in London, all got up in her slipperies and shinies. I described her as much as I could, and he just drove along the straight road, frowning, and shaking his head as if he could hardly believe me.

"Silk two-pieces?" he said. "Spike-heeled shoes? Ten-quid tips?"

"And scent. And bags of make-up. And blue hair. She got her hair done every week."

"I noticed the hair. Gave me a shock. She laughed about it and said it was a bit of fun."

"It was her city side. She probably did it when she lived in Melbourne."

"I've never seen her got up like that," he said.

"You ought to. You'd like it. She looks really fantastic."

He was silent for a while. Trying to picture it, I suppose.

"But all that money, just flung away on rubbish."

"Well, not all of it. On coming to check up on us, because of Dad."

"Yeah, well, course I knew about that, we discussed all *that*. But I thought she'd do it on a shoestring, on a loan from her sister." He shook his head. "Women. You just never know what they're capable of."

He didn't say anything for a long time. I fell asleep when it got dark, but Dave drove right through the night.

When we got to the airport we checked my big case through and then went for a last bite to eat (and a beer for him – he'd been beerless all the way, of course), and he went in to the Body Shop and bought me some beautiful strawberry bath oil.

"You'll like having a bath again, chook," he said.

He hugged me goodbye at the place where everyone has to say goodbye. There were people crying all around, it wasn't only us, so nobody noticed. I liked being hugged by him, he felt so strong and he had a nice smell when he wasn't too sweaty. I thought maybe boys wouldn't be so bad after all, if they could grow up a bit (not as old as Dave, but, you know, have bigger shoulders and protect you and that).

He made sure that I travelled as an unaccompanied minor (that's what it's called when you're under sixteen, we managed to have a laugh over it – miners – get it?!!). One of the airline people had to make sure I got on the plane and let them know at the other end to meet me and see me right.

"How are you going to get home from the airport?" Dave asked.

"On the tube, then the train."

"But you won't manage with all that luggage. You'd better get a taxi."

I promised I would. But the truth was I hadn't any English money, not a penny. I felt all panicky when I thought of that, but I didn't want to tell him – there was nothing he could do about it. I thought maybe the airline person who had to meet me would lend me some.

On the plane I put my emu-egg holdall carefully in the overhead locker and got out my notepad. I looked at my sketch and I thought it was pretty good. When we'd taken off I just scribbled and scribbled and scribbled. I only watched two movies the whole way. One was *Rabbit-Proof Fence* again. I cried more this time because I sort of felt part of their lives – I imagined Merinda being snatched and stuck away in that awful school where they tried to make Wonngai girls lose their roots. I was missing them all already. Australia is so *far*. As the hours went by I kept thinking of that. It was like travelling home from another planet. Would I ever get back to visit them? I didn't let myself think maybe I'd never see them again.

The journey was much worse going back. They kept feeding us till I felt sick and my legs got terribly twitchy as well. If I hadn't had my writing to do I don't know how I'd have got through it. The last three hours seemed like for *ever*.

And I started really getting scared about what I'd do without any money.

We landed at last. It was six-something in the morning UK time but my inner clock thought we were in the middle of some alien time zone. I felt totally, like *totally*, knackered, as if my insides had been squeezed out like toothpaste. As I went through the doorway of the plane I kind of staggered and my bag bumped hard against the edge. I thought I heard a crack. *Oh no*. Not my emu egg!

The person who was meant to meet me because I was an unaccompanied minor never showed up. I stumbled along the passages for miles. The moving walkway was broken (of course). A buggy went by with some old people on it looking as if they'd died. I showed my passport and then walked more miles to the place where the luggage comes through. Everyone standing there looked like zombies.

When my big case with the sunflowers came through the little tunnel, people's faces sort of lit up, it made them laugh. Good old Gran... I dragged it off and put it and my other stuff on one of the trolleys. Then out into the main part of the airport. This was it. Up against the rabbit-proof fence. How was I going to get home with no money?

And there, would you believe it, standing tight to the barrier and waving her arm off, was Mum.

Chapter Fifteen

How did she know?

She knew because Gran'd driven into Cosmo with Dad and they'd phoned her and said I was coming home and when to meet me. And Dad spoke to her and told her he was OK and that he'd write. He even said he loved her, which she'd told me no Aussie blokes ever do. So she was all kind of lit up, and she wasn't in a mood to tell me off or anything.

Gran'd confessed to her that she hadn't meant to send me back but that I'd insisted. That was another reason why instead of getting curry I got half smothered in hugs and kisses.

"Oh, Stace, I'm so glad to see you! I've missed you so much! I've been so miserable and lonely, and I'm in such a mess. Thank you for coming back to me!"

We got on to the tube at Heathrow. We were sitting there all cuddled up and talking like mad when I saw something leaking on to the floor of the train from my holdall. I picked it up quickly. It was from the bottle of bath oil Dave had bought me. *That* was what had broken before! I was so happy it wasn't my emu egg that I didn't even care that everything in my bag was soaked in strawberry oil.

But that turned out to be the least of my worries.

Mum hadn't sold the furniture. She'd borrowed from a loan shark. Some heavies had been round to the flat for the first payment. They came on payday. She'd handed over her wages plus everything she'd had in the Post Office account and gone without food for three days. She'd had to borrow a tenner from the neighbour to come to meet me. She was scared to death.

"They're coming again, and they're going to do something awful, Stacey, I know they are!"

I wanted to ask her what had got into her to borrow money from a stinking mongrel like a loan shark, but what was the use. She'd done it for Dad. And to be totally honest, I was sort of impressed – I mean, that she'd find out how to do something like that, and do it, when everybody knows what those people are like. I mean, brave or what? It was a scary situation to come back to. Mum'd gone back to being helpless. And seriously frightened. The men were coming back in two days. And she hadn't a bean to give them.

We had a conference. I couldn't bear to see her poor, white face, and the way she clenched her hands and kept tearing-up... TLC wasn't in it, I had to keep hugging her and telling her it was all going to be OK. But how?

I rang Nan and asked her what to do. She said, straight off, "Run away," so that's what we did. Nan helped us. She lived way over the other side of London in Hammersmith and we reckoned the heavies wouldn't find us there.

So that first day we – well, me really, jet-lagged out of my head – found a White Van Man in the Yellow Pages, to come round late at night and pack as much of our things as would fit into his van (we helped lug the stuff down the stairs in our building) and drive us across town to Nan's place. Nan called what we did a "midnight flit". She'd done one once, in Shepherd's Bush, when Grandpa couldn't pay the rent. Our furniture wouldn't fit into her little flat so White Van Man said he'd take it to a storage place. Nan whispered that we were crazy and he'd probably run off with it, but next day he came back and me and him and Mum went back to Peckham for the rest of the stuff. We went early in the morning, because it was Heavies Day.

Just as we were driving away with the second lot of stuff, they arrived, looking like undertakers in dark suits in a black car. Mum just pointed into the driving mirror – she went whiter than the van. White Van Man hit the accelerator and shot away like smoke. They jumped back in their car and chased us, but he lost them. He was a *brilliant* driver. He drove us back to Nan's and then took the stuff on to the storage. Nan paid him out of her pension. But he'd only take for one journey and even Nan said what a nice young man.

Well, now the trouble was, Mum had no job of course as she couldn't go back to Peckham and I couldn't go back to my old school, and all this was because Mum couldn't let Dad down. I could easily fill a whole new lot of notepads about this but I mustn't, I've written six full ones already in the past months.

To cut it short, I went to a new school and Mum got a new job. It was at Waitrose this time, the one in Sheen – Mum said she couldn't do her people-guessing game any more because they were pretty well ALL posh, ALL on diets and ALL giving parties (well, that's what Mum said anyway – she's got a good sense of humour, I'll give her that, and we both needed one). We had to wait nearly a year for the council to find us a flat. Nan was so fed up by the time we finally moved out, I bet she wished she'd never taken us in, but there it is, that's what happens when you get into debt. You can't imagine what the storage cost, too, and Nan paid all that for us. Grandmas, eh?

I never did get a computer and I never did catch up at school. Not what you'd call properly, though I do try as hard as I can, and without Loretta to egg me on I don't bunk off any more. I don't know, maybe I've got no head for studying. But I got good at writing. That's my one good thing. And I made some new friends, finally, though I still miss Loretta. I suppose I know now that she wasn't exactly – you know. I mean, she could've got me into a load of bother. But she was a good laugh.

One thing I have to write is letters, to keep in touch with Gran and Dave and Dad. You want to know how they solved *their* little problems?

Well. The mining company never took Gran to court. Their witness, if there was one, went walkabout and they had no proof, so they just gave up on the thirty thousand dollars.

For the rest, I bet you'll never guess. Or maybe you will. After all he'd said about greedy miners, Dave caught gold fever.

It seems he kept thinking about that strike at the Lady Bountiful mine, that river of pure gold that you couldn't break with a 'dozer. He got Gran to sell some of the cattle. She was dead against it but he stood right up to her and insisted. He bought a big digger second-hand from Harvey at Cosmo, and started drilling and digging on the other side of the Aboriginal sacred waterhole, just in case there *was* an ancient underground river of gold that ran right on beyond it. He called it the Stacey Mine. Yeah! I've got a gold mine named after me. I must say, I liked that a lot. He hasn't struck it rich yet, but he did find *some* gold. He sent me a tiny leather bag with a couple of little nuggets in it for my fifteenth birthday.

Poor Gran. With Dave gone gold-crazy, the only person she had to help her on the station was Dad. And here's a major, *major* surprise. He came good.

Well. Not right away. At first he just kept skiving off, taking the Toyota and going into town to go boozing with some of his old mates. But then one day, when he got back, he found the yard full of cows and Gran lying on the veranda, collapsed – I mean unconscious. She'd been trying to do a muster – that's what they call it when they round up the cattle for market – by herself.

This gave Dad a real wake-up call. Because she'd had a bit of a heart attack. He had to radio for the Flying Doctor! It sounds awful, but I wish I'd been there for that – the plane flying in on to my landing strip where I'd learnt to drive. They flew her to hospital in a place called Kalgoorlie. She soon got better, but while she was away, Dad and Dave had a real set-to. It nearly ended in them punching each other's lights out, because they both blamed each other, but in the end they decided that for Gran's sake they had to make peace, and Dad decided for himself that if he was going to live on the station, he had to pull his weight. Dave offered to give up the mine but they decided he ought to go on with it, because it's the only hope they have of ever getting some real money.

The interesting thing was, when Dad got down to it he found out he likes ranching, or stationing, or whatever you'd call it. There's not all that much to do, except in spurts, and keeping the windmills working and stuff wasn't too stressful, not like keeping a nine-to-five job in England, which he'd been hopeless at. He and Dave began to get on together (they both like their beer and sport on the radio, and neither of them talks much, so they were quite happy on the station). The thing was, they both pitched in to help Gran, even though as soon as she was better she tried to do everything the same as always. Dad wrote he practically had to tie her to her precious gantry to keep her from working. Dad even did the housework and some of the cooking (though I think that wasn't a major success, but at least there were no salads!).

Sometimes, when they have some dosh, Dad sends us some. That's how we paid Nan back. He always writes a letter to go with the money. Mum just lives for those letters. There was a time when I wished she'd get over him, but I don't any more. I just dream and plan for how we could go over there, the two of us, and maybe Dad and Mum might get together again. At least there are no slappers on the station. Even Aussie men have to dream, and I think he dreams about being back with Mum, his Rock of Gibraltar (would you believe his nickname for her is Rocky? *She loves it*).

There's been some upgrading at the station. They set up the phone box again, the one that runs by solar panels and got blown over by the tornado, and Dad, who's handier than you'd think, took the first real bit of gold-money, drove into town and came back with a satellite dish and a TV set. So now the men have footie and cricket on the box, and Gran's got email, and that's the main way I write to them (I can email from school).

I nagged and nagged Dave in my letters about Roo and in the end he went into Cosmo to find out about her. Merinda wasn't there, she'd gone bush with her family, but Harvey – who's the local big cheese – said she didn't have her any more. He said Roo'd gone walkabout. Dave wrote that to be honest, he thought they might have eaten her. But he didn't tell me that until after he found out they hadn't.

Because one day she just came bouncing back to the homestead! Everyone gave her a great welcome. She'd got her own joey and Dad bought a cheap camera and sent me photos of her. I keep them stuck in my dressing-table mirror behind my emu egg. (I've got my own room at our new flat, thank God. While we were at Nan's I had to doss down on the sofa and Mum slept in with Nan. There was one good thing on the side, though. Nan wouldn't stand for Mum smoking in her flat so Mum had to give up, and she hasn't started again, at least not so far. She doesn't even chew gum like Gran either, she just wears these patches on her arm. I keep telling her how much nicer she smells.)

Because I'd left my old school I couldn't tell my friends about how I could drive and how I'd saved my dad. I tried to, at the new school, but nobody believed me and they thought I was showing off, so I just shut up. Mum believed me. She and Nan made me tell the story of my Epic Drive about fifty times and they said I was a heroine. Which was good to hear.

But you know what I think? I think a heroine's somebody who can just live like we do and not go under or get into trouble, like Loretta might, and like Dad did and like Mum did. When I told Nan this idea she said I was right.

"You have to be tough," she said. "Tough, but straight. And you have to have a laugh. That's the long and short of it."

I think Nan might like the Aussies, because they're sort of like that.

* * *

There's just one more thing before I finish off. My scorpion totem. I couldn't find him in the sky in London because, for one thing, there's so much light all around you, you can't hardly see any stars. So one night, I got Mum to walk with me across Hammersmith Bridge and down on the towpath by the river, where there's no electric light. We found a place without too many trees, and I stared up at the sky for ages, looking for my scorpion, and Mum looked too, but he still wasn't there. I suppose it's because we're in the northern hemisphere. He must be round the other side of the sky (is that right? Mum didn't know either). But Mum said that wherever he is, he's still my totem animal and he's still part of me, like everything I saw and did and thought about in Oz is still part of me, even if I never go back there.

But I will. I definitely will. I've made it my priority.

I got this email from Gran. I was really excited! A special website for my outback adventure, and my life, really...

From: yamarna@bigpond.net.au
To: stacey@lynnereidbanks.com
Subject: Stealing Stacey Website

Hi pet!

I'm getting really hot on websites, and I've made one specially for you, with loads of photos to remind you of Yamarna and your stay in the outback.

It's got different pages, including some of the photos I took in London of Peckham and your old school, so it illustrates all your notebook that you told me about.

Love from Gran.

PS I like the ones of Humpy best!

www.lynnereidbanks.com/stealingstacey